"Would you try to deny that you want me?"

A tremor ran the length of her spine. She stiffened in his arms, fighting to regain control of her senses. "This is contemptible," she whispered. "Let go of me, Rafael!"

"Not until you give me an answer," he said. "A truthful answer."

"All right!" The words were torn from her. "So I want you. It's purely physical, and I hate myself for it. Now, will you let me go?"

There was a suspended moment when he made no move; then he dropped his arms, allowing her to draw away from him.

"I may not be able to control the way I feel but I can control the way I act. Even if you weren't attempting to steal my children from me, do you really think I'd enter into any kind of sexual liaison with my husband's brother?"

KAY THORPE, an English author, has always been able to spin a good yarn. In fact, her teachers said she was the best storyteller in the school—particularly with excuses for being late! Kay then explored a few unsatisfactory career paths before giving rein to her imagination and hitting the jackpot with her first romance novel. After a roundabout route, she'd found her niche at last. The author, who lives with her husband and son in Derbyshire, enjoys reading, hiking and traveling.

Books by Kay Thorpe

HARLEQUIN PRESENTS

1501—TROUBLE ON TOUR
1534—LASTING LEGACY
1556—WILD STREAK
1571—LEFT IN TRUST
1603—PAST ALL REASON
1619—THE ALPHA MAN

HARLEQUIN ROMANCE

2151—TIMBER BOSS
2232—THE WILDERNESS TRAIL
2234—FULL CIRCLE

KAY
THORPE

The Spanish Connection

Harlequin Books

TORONTO • NEW YORK • LONDON
AMSTERDAM • PARIS • SYDNEY • HAMBURG
STOCKHOLM • ATHENS • TOKYO • MILAN
MADRID • WARSAW • BUDAPEST • AUCKLAND

ISBN 0-373-11667-5

THE SPANISH CONNECTION

This edition published by arrangement with Harlequin Enterprises B. V.

Printed in U.S.A.

CHAPTER ONE

LOOKING back through the rear screen as they drove east along the coastal road, at the massive pile of grey rock framed against the cloudless sky, Lauren could see why it had been known to the ancient world as the Pillar of Hercules. It was difficult to believe that over thirty thousand people lived and worked in that small area. Seen from the air, the whole of Gibraltar occupied no more than two or three square miles.

César and Nicolás were fast asleep on the back seat of the luxurious limousine, dark heads close together, faces angelic in repose. More of Francisco than herself in those twin sets of well defined features, Lauren was bound to acknowledge.

If she had anything at all to do with it, those looks would be all that the two of them would inherit of their father. They were English by birth; their Spanish blood made no difference to that. Accepting Rafael's invitation to visit the Javierre de Quiros estate in no way undermined her determination to retain their independence.

Rafael. A fancy name indeed for the kind of man Francisco had described. Not that the latter had turned out to be any paragon of virtue. Five years of marriage to a man who saw no reason to confine his sexual activities to one woman was enough to destroy every last vestige of love—if love it had ever really been.

Settling back into her seat, she stole a swift glance at the young man driving the car. Gabriel had those same devil-may-care good looks that had attracted her so wildly to Francisco, yet they did absolutely nothing to her heartstrings right now. 'Call me Angel,' he had said with a grin at the airport, 'and I'll call you little sister because I'm one year older than you.' That made him twenty-five—ten years younger than Rafael, four between him and Francisco. His brother's death didn't appear to have affected him very badly. But then why should he mourn for a man he'd neither seen nor heard from in so long a time? Blood wasn't necessarily thicker than water.

'Rafael would have come to meet you himself,' he said now, sensing her glance, 'but he had business matters to attend. You know, of course, of the Quiros hotels?'

Lauren shook her head. 'I know very little about family matters.'

It was Gabriel's turn to cast a glance, lingering for a long moment on the pure oval of her face and heavy rope of honey-gold hair. 'You're a Quiros yourself now.'

Green eyes darkened a fraction. 'Only by marriage. I've no intention of claiming any personal involvement.'

'As Francisco's widow, you're one of the family. Rafael will insist on treating you as such.'

'Even though he and Francisco were estranged for so many years?'

'It was Francisco's own choice to leave. He had no great love for anyone but himself.'

An accurate summary, Lauren reflected. Francisco hadn't even loved the twins the way any normal father would. To him they had represented a responsibility he could well have lived without. If it hadn't been for her pregnancy he would never have married her at all; she was only too well aware of that. She supposed she should be grateful for the fact that he had possessed at least a modicum of decency.

Meeting the handsome Spaniard at a party when she was nineteen, she had been totally bowled over by his rakish dark looks and confident manner. Francisco Javierre de Quiros—his very name had been a draw. The fact that he had appeared to be equally bowled over by her hadn't helped her to keep a clear head. Within a week they had become lovers; three months later they were married: a register office affair, with only her closest friend in attendance. Francisco had refused to inform his brothers either of the marriage itself or the subsequent birth of their nephews. That had been left to her after the accident which had robbed her of a husband and the twins of a father—and only then after going through his papers to discover their whereabouts.

The invitation to visit had come by return of post, couched in terms she had found a little offputting at first in their formality. The costs would naturally be met, Rafael had advised. All the same, Lauren had left it several months before finally making up her mind to accept.

'Do you really live in a castle?' she asked now.

Gabriel smiled. 'Only a part of one. The other part is run as a hotel. A very exclusive hotel, of course,' he added. 'No more than a dozen guests at a time, and those out of the top drawer, as you would say.'

Lauren laughed. 'Your English is top-class too.'

'I learn good,' he said, momentarily destroying the illusion. 'Rafael speaks French and German also.'

'He must be very clever,' Lauren commented, eliciting a shrug.

'Some have the ear for other languages. I'm content with the English. Perhaps one day I'll visit your country myself.'

'That would be nice,' she said. 'You could come and stay with us.'

There was an odd expression in the dark eyes turned fleetingly towards her, a certain evasiveness in his answer. 'Perhaps.'

Thronged with traffic, the road took much of his attention over the following hour or so. He drove too fast for Lauren's comfort, but she couldn't bring herself to remonstrate with someone she had only just met, brother-in-law or not. She concentrated instead on the passing scenery, from fertile coastal plain to the rugged heights where lay their eventual destination. A castle in Spain. It had such a romantic sound to it.

Francisco had never told her just why he had felt moved to leave his home and country, but the family rift had obviously been a very bad one. He had hated Rafael. Perhaps the latter would be prepared to tell her why. She needed to understand.

Estepona came and went. Lauren had read of the beautiful harbour there, but could see no sign of it from the road, just a long stretch of beach fronted by hotels and shops. With the season not yet into its stride, the tourist element wasn't too obtrusive, although the sun was already hot enough to make her grateful for the air-conditioned comfort of the car.

It would be cooler up in the sierras, of course, especially in the evenings. She had brought sweaters for the boys, and a couple of light jackets for herself, just in case. Not that she intended their stay to be a lengthy one. She was here only because Rafael had asked her to come, and because she thought it only right for

Francisco's brothers to at least see their nephews. Curiosity had played a part too, she was bound to admit.

Some short time later, they turned away from the coast to start the climb towards Ronda. The road was narrow and winding, the traffic sparse, the emerging scenery breathtaking. A low crash barrier was the only protection against the increasingly steep drops to the left. Coming down again would be worse, Lauren thought, with the passenger-seat closest to the edge. For anyone like herself, who found the top deck of a bus too high for comfort, the thought alone was daunting. Odd that she suffered no sense of vertigo on a plane.

Ronda lay sprawled across a gently sloping plateau, the golden stone of its walled old quarter offset by the sparkling white of the slightly more modern stretch. Lauren cowered down in her seat as they drove across the bridge spanning the fearful depths of the gorge which split the town in two, although she could actually glimpse little of the actual drop from the car.

Prisoners, Gabriel informed her, had at one time been held in cells contained within the central span. With a three-hundred-foot plunge right outside the windows, there could, Lauren conceded, have been few prisons more secure.

Some fifteen minutes or so beyond the town, they turned off once more on to an even narrower road. The mountains were all about them now, softened by the lowering sun. The grass up here was emerald-green, the air itself crystal-clear, the whole landscape magnificent. A different Spain altogether from the general tourist impression, reflected Lauren.

Her first glimpse of the castle was awe-inspiring. Built of the same warm stone as the old Ronda township, it sat in a commanding position overlooking a sweeping amphitheatre of a valley. The high square turrets and castellated walls looked as solid and impregnable as the day they had been erected. There was even a portcullis spanning the entrance archway, she noted as they approached, raised at present but still in use if one were to judge from its appearance in passing beneath.

It was closed each night for total security, Gabriel confirmed, though from what or whom she was left to guess.

The twins awoke as the car came to a halt in the big square courtyard.

'Is this the castle?' asked Nicolás, hoisting himself upright to look out of the window. 'It wasn't very far.'

'This is it,' Lauren confirmed. 'You slept the whole way here, that's why it didn't seem to take long.'

She got out of the car to open the rear door, steadying the two of them as they tumbled eagerly out. 'Best behaviour, remember,' she warned them, only too well aware of the havoc they could wreak between them if not kept in strict check. It was quite normal for twins to be more mischievous than most, she had been assured by numerous people, simply because there were two of them together. And especially boys. She could only hope that Rafael would prove tolerant where children were concerned, and not expect too much. Seen but not heard was all very well in theory; in practice the 'but not' tended to be replaced by 'and'.

'Your luggage will be brought in,' said Gabriel. 'Rafael will be waiting to meet you.'

'I thought you said he was out on business?' Lauren queried.

'His car is here,' indicating a low-slung coupé parked under the lee of a wall alongside several more vehicles, 'so he must be too. He will have hurried matters along in order to be back for your arrival.'

Lauren would have much preferred the time and opportunity for a shower and change of clothing before meeting her other brother-in-law, but didn't like to suggest it. Given its function as an exclusive hotel, the castle had to have every mod con installed.

'You'd better lead on, then,' she said resignedly.

She took one small hand firmly in each of hers as they entered through the iron-clad door into a large vaulted hall. The floor beneath her feet would in all probability be stone-flagged like the courtyard outside, she guessed, but it was carpeted now in deep ruby-red with pile so thick that her heels sank right in. The walls were stone, though hardly bare, their length and much of their height festooned with displays of armour and painted battle scenes, the latter interspersed with ancient portraits of high-ranking military personnel. The heavily carved dark wood table stretching almost the full length of the room held a huge centre-piece in what was surely solid silver, while above the great open fireplace hung a silver shield bearing what Lauren took to be the family crest.

'I didn't realise you had a military background,' she commented as Gabriel made for a door at the far end of the hall.

'It ended two generations ago,' he replied, 'but it is a source of some pride still. Our ancestors fought many famous battles. I brought you through this way in order to show you the splendour, but our private quarters have a separate entrance which you should use in the future. You and the children are to sleep in the east tower. You'll find the views from your rooms very good.'

Lauren was sure of it. The views from any angle could only be spectacular. If the rest of the castle was of the same standard as that she had seen up to now, the hotel must rank among the finest in the country.

The door gave on to an inner hall somewhat smaller than the first. A fine carved staircase rose to an open gallery. Gabriel made for another door to the left marked 'private', ushering the three of them through ahead of him. The short corridor beyond was also carpeted. It in turn opened out into yet another small hall.

Quiet up until now, César tugged at Lauren's hand. 'I'm thirsty,' he declared.

'Me too,' claimed Nicolás promptly.

'Just a few minutes more,' Lauren promised, hoping it would be no more than that. 'We're going to see your other uncle now.'

'I don't want to,' said César mutinously. 'I want to go home.'

'Me too,' Nicolás agreed. 'When are we going home, Mummy?'

'We only just got here.' Lauren glanced apologetically at Gabriel. 'It's been a long day for them.'

'Perhaps it would be better if you meet with Rafael alone for now,' he suggested. 'I'll take them to find a drink and something to eat.'

Expecting protests, Lauren was surprised when neither boy hesitated in taking the hands Gabriel held out to them. Ranged together, the family resemblance was unmistakable. Lauren knew a sudden inexplicable sense of foreboding—a feeling that she alone was the outsider here.

'Rafael will be in the *salón*,' Gabriel advised. 'That door over there. I'll bring the children back in half an hour.'

Left alone, she took a deep breath before opening the door indicated, to find herself in a large and airy room lit by three tall windows. The walls in here were plastered plain white and hung with more portraits and landscapes, the furnishings heavy and ornate. The man seated on one of the vast sofas flanking an even vaster fireplace came lithely to his feet on her entry, dropping the sheaf of papers he had been studying on to a side-table.

Rafael was an inch or two taller than either of his brothers at around six feet, shoulders broad and powerful, hips lean. He was clad in plain black shirt and trousers, the former open at the throat to reveal a glint of gold from the small medallion nestled there. Facially, he possessed the same devastating bone-structure, the same sensuous line of mouth, yet the jaunty quality shared by both Francisco and Gabriel was missing, replaced by what Lauren could only describe to herself as arrogance. She felt an instant and purely instinctive antipathy.

'I trust you had a comfortable journey?' he said.

'Very, thank you,' she replied formally. 'It was good of you to make all the arrangements.'

One dark eyebrow lifted. 'I'd scarcely have left you to make your own.'

'Oh, I'm quite capable,' she declared. 'English women are used to doing things for themselves.'

'Doubtless.' His tone was dry. 'This, however, is not England.' Eyes as black as coal appraised her, moving with deliberation from her face to take in every detail of her slim though shapely figure in the beige trouser suit. 'Francisco showed remarkably good taste,' he observed. 'You're not at all what I anticipated.'

'And what was that?' Lauren asked.

He shrugged dismissively. 'It's of no importance now. I take it that you left the children with Gabriel?'

'They were thirsty,' she said. 'It's been a long journey for them.'

The dark head inclined. 'Of course. In the meantime, we have a great deal to discuss.' He indicated the sofa from which he had risen. 'Please make yourself comfortable. You would like something to drink yourself, perhaps?'

Lauren shook her head, moving forward to perch self-consciously on the very edge of the sofa and as far away as possible from the man still standing. 'Not at the moment, thanks.'

'To eat, then?'

'I'm not hungry.'

'We eat our main meal of the day very late by your standards,' Rafael advised. 'I'll have something light brought to you between times. The children, of course, will take their meal at a time suited to their retirement.' He paused, making no attempt to take a seat himself. 'You said in your letter that Francisco left provision enough for the three of you. That was less than the truth, I believe?'

Lauren bit her lip. 'You've been making enquiries about us?'

'There was a need,' he agreed imperturbably. 'How else was I to know that your claim was genuine?'

'I'm not here to make any claim!' she denied. 'We have a home of our own, and an income adequate to our needs.'

'A home mortgaged up to the limit and an income scarcely adequate to cover the repayments, much less anything else,' came the unmoved response. 'Francisco left Spain with capital sufficient to provide security for the rest of his life if wisely invested, but there is, I gather, little of it left. From where, may I ask, will come money for education, to name but one future requirement?'

'Education,' Lauren answered tautly, 'is free in England.'

'Not the kind I'm speaking of. Unless, of course, you wish less than the best for your sons?'

'Of course I don't. No mother would!'

'In which case, you have little choice but to accept assistance from the only family you have.'

Lauren was silent for a long moment. 'You really have been doing some research, haven't you?' she said at length.

'I know that you were brought up in a children's home from the age of twelve after your parents were killed,' he agreed. 'I also know how hard you worked to make something of your life after leaving the home at eighteen. But for meeting my brother, you might well have succeeded. Judging from the date of your marriage, and that of the birth, conception took place some two months prior to the event. You were fortunate not to be left holding the baby, as it were.'

'Oh, very.' Lauren made no attempt to iron the bitterness from her voice. 'Is there anything you don't know?'

'I'm aware that there were other women during the course of your marriage,' he said. 'I would have anticipated no less from my brother. No doubt he never told you the true reason why he left Spain?'

Green eyes met black, holding the penetrating gaze with an effort. 'All I know is that there was some kind of disagreement between the two of you.'

The strong mouth twisted. 'That is one way of putting it.' The pause was weighted. 'Did you love him?'

Lauren looked down at the hands locked in her lap. 'I thought I did.'

'But not ultimately?'

She swallowed on the hard lump in her throat. 'I don't suppose so.'

'He killed whatever it was that you did feel for him, yes?'

'Yes.' The word was dragged from her. She rallied her emotions to add, 'I don't really see where this is getting us. The failure was as much my fault as his.'

'I doubt that. Francisco was incapable of staying faithful to any one woman. You were not the first to be impregnated by him. Six years ago he took the seventeen-year-old daughter of one of our oldest family friends.'

Lauren felt numb. 'What happened to her?'

'She underwent a back-street abortion arranged by Francisco, and bled to death.'

The lack of emotionalism in the deep-timbred voice in no way lessened the horror of the telling. Lauren gazed at him with darkened eyes, unable to think of a single thing to say.

'I had no idea,' she managed at last.

'Hardly a story he was going to impart to you himself. He suggested no such course to you?'

'No.'

'Then his feelings for you must have gone somewhat deeper than was usual with him. Initially, at least.' Rafael studied her with an unreadable expression. 'I'm sorry to be the one to tell you all this, but it was necessary for you to know the truth.'

'It gives you even less reason to consider yourself in any way responsible for my and the twins' welfare,' Lauren murmured thickly.

'The sins of the fathers cannot be visited upon the sons—nor those of the husband upon the wife. Who else is there to be responsible for your welfare?' He held up a staying hand as she opened her mouth to speak. 'There is nothing more to be said on the subject.'

Lauren spread her hands in a helpless little gesture, her resentment at his summary dismissal tempered by the knowledge that he was right about future security. She had spoken the truth when she said she could manage, but it was only just. If not for herself, she owed it to the twins to accept the situation.

But only providing, she vowed, that Rafael didn't attempt to take over too much of their lives.

Watching him now as he moved to open a dark wood cabinet and extract glasses, she wondered why he was still unmarried himself. It certainly couldn't be through lack of opportunity. Lack of desire to be tied, perhaps? All the same, he was of an age when some decision surely had to be made if he wanted a son and heir of his own.

Taking the glass of sherry from him, she was aware of a tingle like a small electric shock as their fingers momentarily came into contact. Hardly surprising, she thought, trying not to let anything show in her face. Few women could fail to be affected by such sheer male magnetism. Francisco had exuded it too, if on a rather different plane.

'To the future,' Rafael toasted, eyes locked on to hers.

'The future,' she echoed, and felt once again that faint sense of foreboding.

Gabriel's arrival with the twins was something of a relief. Obviously tired from the journey, they were uncharacteristically subdued. Nicolás stuck his thumb in his mouth and refused to speak when greeted by his senior uncle—a habit Lauren had believed him cured of some time ago. César too was overawed enough to stick close to his mother's skirts.

'Had there been any doubt at all in my mind of their parentage, it would be dispelled now,' Rafael acknowledged, looking from one to the other. 'They very much resemble their father.'

'In looks,' agreed Lauren shortly, 'if not in manner. I think it might be a good idea if we went and unpacked. They're usually in bed by seven.' She forbore from mentioning that sleep rarely came before nine.

'But of course.' Rafael glanced at his brother. 'Gabriel will show you the way. I look forward to seeing you again at dinner.'

Rising to her feet, Lauren hesitated before saying tentatively, 'Would it be too impolite of me to take advantage of an early night myself? It's been rather a long day for us all.'

There was no telling anything from Rafael's expression, though his nod was somewhat perfunctory. 'As you prefer. A light meal will be brought to you in one hour from now. I trust you will find your rooms satisfactory.'

'I'm sure of it,' she said. She paused, not at all sure how to take her leave of him, tagging on lamely, 'I'll say goodnight, then.'

Just for a moment there was a gleam almost of amusement in the dark eyes. 'Goodnight, Lauren.'

Her name on his lips sounded different—exotic almost. She felt a sudden tremor run through her. With the twins ranged alongside, she followed Gabriel from the room, aware the whole way across the wide expanse of floor of Rafael's gaze on her departing back, and unnerved by the knowledge.

She must have drawn an audible breath of relief when they reached the hall again, for Gabriel looked at her with a certain understanding.

'My brother can be intimidating,' he said, 'but he means what he says. Neither you nor the boys will ever want for anything again. Of that you can be assured.'

'That isn't why I'm here,' Lauren protested for what seemed the umpteenth time. 'There's more to life than money!'

'But little comfort without it.' Gabriel moved across to open an arched door beyond which a narrow staircase spiralled out of sight. 'I'm afraid we don't have any lifts, but it's only the next floor. Rafael thought the higher rooms would be too far for the children.'

Not just the children, Lauren could have told him. The castle was elevated to start with. From the top of the tower, the ground must look a mile away. The boys, thank heaven, didn't appear to have inherited her fear of heights. If anything, they were a little too daring. At four years of age, they knew nothing of the laws of gravity as yet.

The stairs gave on to a central landing with three doors opening from it. Two bedrooms, with a smaller room converted to a bathroom between. Lauren was rendered speechless by the magnificence of the four-poster bed in the room she was to occupy. With a mattress level at least three feet from the floor, she would need to take a running jump to make it, she reflected.

The boys' room had modern twin divans, much to her relief. Brought in specially for them, Gabriel informed her when she remarked on the difference in style of furnishings.

'Rafael's idea,' he said. 'He thought the original furnishings unsuitable for children of their years. This was my room when I was a boy, while Francisco had the one you're occupying. Rafael has the upper floor to himself still.'

'You haven't turned out just for us, have you?' Lauren asked anxiously.

Gabriel laughed and shook his head. 'I chose to move my sleeping quarters years ago. Not that it would have been any penance. You can't know how much I've looked forward to your coming. To think that Francisco kept you such a secret all these years!'

A fact he hadn't been all that keen on acknowledging to anyone, Lauren could have told him, but refrained. Francisco was dead and gone. Why further debase his memory?

The luggage had already been brought up, the two cases unpacked and everything put tidily away in cupboards and drawers. One of the nightdresses Lauren had brought was laid out ready on the bed in her room. White and sheer, it drew Gabriel's eyes like a magnet.

One of the few presents Francisco had ever bought her. White for virginity, he had said satirically at the time, because she was still a virgin at heart. She had never worn it up to now, but it was too lovely and expensive a garment to discard out of hand.

'I'm going to have difficulty climbing up on to that bed,' she said with a laugh in an effort to dispel the memories. 'You don't happen to have a ladder handy, do you?'

'You'll find a wooden step underneath for the purpose,' Gabriel replied, taking her seriously. 'Do you need help in preparing the boys for their bedtime? One of the staff can be alerted.'

'No, thanks, I can manage fine,' she assured him. 'I always have up to now.' She gave him a smile. 'We'll see you in the morning, then. What time is breakfast?'

'The hotel guests are served between eight and nine,' he said. 'Rafael prefers to take his meal no later than seven-thirty, but you have no need to follow suit. If you wish for something more substantial than coffee and bread rolls or *churros*, there is a wide choice available.'

'Just cereals for the boys, perhaps. I'll be quite happy with coffee and rolls.'

'I'll tell the kitchen.' Gabriel added, 'And tomorrow I'll show you the whole place.'

'That will be nice.' Lauren made a move towards the door. 'I'd better go and check on what those two are up to. They're too quiet for comfort.'

The boys were quiet, she found, because they were both of them sound asleep, curled up on their respective beds without a care in the world. Too cruel to disturb them now, she thought fondly, gazing down at the twin faces. Baths would simply have to wait until morning.

'I'll just take their shoes off and leave them,' she murmured to Gabriel who was hovering in the doorway. 'They're not going to come to any harm sleeping in their clothes for once.'

'No harm at all,' he agreed. He waited until she had emerged from the room and closed the door softly behind her to add, 'You are a very caring mother, Lauren. And a very beautiful one too. I envy Francisco the five years he spent with you.'

There was a caution in her smile. 'You need never envy anyone anything, Gabriel. Goodnight.'

He accepted the dismissal with obvious reluctance. 'Goodnight.'

Left alone at last, Lauren went back into her own room and closed the door, standing for a moment in silent contemplation. Three brothers, all so different. Gabriel might resemble Francisco the most in actual looks, but his was by far the softer personality. That he was attracted to her was more than apparent; he hadn't even attempted to conceal the fact. She was going to need to be careful in the way she handled their relationship.

Rafael was another matter altogether. In some ways he frightened her. Not a physical fear, more an inner disturbance. She had a strong feeling that her stay here was going to prove anything but tranquil.

CHAPTER TWO

FIRST light came just before seven, turning the sky from black to pale grey then spreading blue. Watching from her window, Lauren thought she had never seen anything quite so beautiful as the mountains sprang into sharp silhouette, taking on colour and detail by degrees. The air was clean and sharp. She drew in deep breaths of it. A couple of weeks of this couldn't be anything but good.

The boys had been up and about for over an hour. It was only with difficulty that she had restrained them from running riot. They were occupied now with the painting books and crayons she had brought with her from home, but the interest wouldn't last too long. Inquisitive by nature, the two needed constant stimulation. Lauren had taught them both to read, and was justifiably proud of their prowess. With luggage limited, however, she had been unable to bring along too much in the way of reading matter, and local shops were unlikely to hold a great stock of children's literature in the English language. Boredom spelled trouble with a capital T where the twins were concerned.

At half-past seven, with the sun just creeping over the eastern range, she took the two of them downstairs. All was silent in the hallway, all doors leading from it closed. Lauren chose the one next to the room she had been in the previous evening, to find herself in what was obviously a study-cum-library. César and Nicolás eyed the crowded bookshelves with interest, undeterred by the man who rose from his seat at the big dark wood desk. Dressed this morning in cream trousers and dark brown shirt, he was no less disturbing.

'I'm sorry,' said Lauren hastily. 'I was looking for the dining-room.'

'No matter,' Rafael assured her. 'The *comedor* is across the other side of the hall. Whatever you wish to eat, you have only to ask. We cater for all tastes.'

'Just cereals,' she responded. 'For the twins, that is. We never eat anything cooked at breakfast.'

'No more than we do ourselves.' He glanced at the twins as they prowled along the nearest shelves. 'Do you speak any Spanish at all?'

'Only a word or two.' Lauren had her eyes on the boys too. 'Francisco rarely used it himself.'

'Perhaps because he was all too rarely present to do so,' came the dry return, bringing her gaze sharply back to the olive-skinned features.

'What's that supposed to mean?'

'You know what it means,' he said. 'I've made it my duty since first discovering your existence to explore every aspect of my brother's lifestyle during these past years. He was, it seems, no family man. He pursued other interests.'

Neither César nor Nicolás appeared to be listening to the conversation, but Lauren knew them too well to be assured that they were taking none of it in. No matter what his faults, Francisco was their father. She wanted them to remember the good times, few though they had been, rather than those of neglect.

'I think we'd better go and have breakfast,' she said. 'We've disturbed you long enough.'

'No matter,' Rafael repeated. 'By the time you finish your meal, I'll have finished my work. The children will be taken care of while I show you over the castle.'

'Gabriel was going to do that,' she claimed, and saw the firm mouth take on a slant.

'Gabriel has other commitments today. He left for Málaga half an hour ago. This afternoon I thought you might care to visit Ronda—unless, of course, you'd prefer to take siesta? A custom I've little time for myself, but I have no objection to others following it.'

Lauren shook her head. 'I'm not used to resting during the day either.'

His nod approved the reply. 'The children, of course, will follow their usual routine. The nursemaid who will be supervising them is a very trustworthy young woman. You can leave them safely in her hands.'

'Nursemaid?' Lauren was too angry at the presumption to pay heed to listening ears. 'That's hardly necessary!'

Dark brows lifted. 'You'd prefer that they were left to their own devices?'

'They'll hardly be that when I'm here with them.'

'But you need time of your own to do the things you enjoy,' Rafael stated firmly.

Faced with two pairs of eyes alert to the altered atmosphere in the room, Lauren bit down hard on the response trembling on her lips. 'We'll discuss this later,' she said instead, low-toned.

'By all means,' he agreed.

'Were you and Uncle Rafael quarrelling?' asked César in his clear treble as they went from the room.

'No, of course not,' Lauren denied, too well aware that Rafael could hear every word. 'Just talking, that's all.'

'About us,' piped up Nicolás, not to be left out. 'We're going to have a nursemaid to play with!'

Lauren closed the door firmly behind her before answering that one. 'I'll play with you myself.'

'But you're going out with Uncle Rafael,' said César, sounding not in the least concerned at the notion. 'Nico and me are going to splore.'

'Explore,' Lauren corrected automatically. 'And you don't go anywhere on your own. There are people staying here who won't want children under their feet.'

'Don't they like children?' asked Nicolás.

'Well, yes, of course they do. At least, I imagine so. It's just that they're unlikely to be the kind of people who...' Lauren sighed and came to a floundering halt, sensing the pitfalls inherent in that line of explanation. 'They're paying guests here on holiday,' she substituted. 'This isn't the kind of place you'd bring children to.'

'You brought us,' César pointed out with indisputable logic.

'That's different.'

He considered for a moment before asking the anticipated, 'Why?'

'Because it is,' Lauren responded firmly, in no mood for an extended session. Their having intelligence quotients above the normal for their age level was all very well, but supplying rational answers to the ever-ready questions sometimes taxed her to the limit. Hyper-activity was the result of a mind over-stimulated by its thirst for knowledge, the child psychologist, whom she had consulted on the advice of her GP, had said. It would lessen as that need was appeased.

Their starting school in September would help, although she was going to miss the pair of them like crazy. Still, it would leave her free to take at least a part-time job—always providing she could find one, of course. One thing she had no intention of doing was relying on Rafael for total support.

By comparison with the other rooms she had seen, the *comedor* could almost be described as intimate. The table, Lauren reckoned, would seat no more than a dozen at full stretch. Packets of cereal were ranged alongside a selection of preserves and jugs of orange juice on a side-table. As she helped the boys make their choice, a door on the far side of the room opened to admit a youngish woman wearing a neat blue dress and carrying a basket of rolls along with an earthenware coffee-pot.

'*Buenos días, señora*,' she said pleasantly.

Lauren smiled and returned the greeting, deploring her accent. 'I'm afraid I don't speak your language,' she apologised.

'I speak English,' said the other. 'It is needed that we do so for the guests. My name is María. The coffee is freshly made, the rolls warm from the oven. Is there anything else I can fetch for you, *señora*?'

'No, this is just fine,' Lauren assured her. 'Thank you, María.'

The woman smiled and withdrew. Seated at table, the twins polished off their cereal in short order and had two rolls apiece spread with apricot preserve. Neither of them was over-fond of coffee, but they made vast inroads into the orange juice. Freshly squeezed, Lauren had been quick to note. Everything here would be top-class, of course. The kind of guests who could afford to stay in such surroundings would expect nothing less than the best.

The view from the windows was the same one she had from her own room. With the sun now well up in the sky, the light was pure and sparkling, the distances needle-sharp. Gazing out, she knew an eagerness to be out there exploring the beckoning beauty of the Sierra.

Rafael himself was the only drawback. There was no relaxing in his presence; she felt tense again at the very thought of him. Accustomed to ruling the roost, there was no doubt, but he needn't think he was going to do it with her. She would go along with his plans for the twins' care and entertainment at the moment because they themselves seemed willing enough to be left, only no way was she going to abdicate from her position as parent in ultimate charge.

With breakfast over, and the boys already restless, she was at something of a loss as to where to go from here. Emerging once more into the hall, she thought at first that the beautiful dark-haired young woman, just emerging from the library with Rafael at her back, was one of the guests who had perhaps lost her way, an idea soon scotched when he introduced her as Elena Santos who would be taking care of the children.

'I am very happy to have such a task,' said the girl. 'I will be very careful of their welfare, *señora*.' She smiled at the two boys. 'You would like to play a game with me?'

They answered in unison and in the affirmative, apparently quite happy themselves with the arrangement. Lauren stifled a pang as they went off without a backward glance. Such parting was something she was going to have to accept anyway when they started school, and the sooner she got used to it the better. They couldn't spend their whole lives tied to her apron strings; she wouldn't want them to.

'Which leaves the two of us free to follow our own pursuits,' declared Rafael. 'You would like to see the rest of the castle?'

'I don't want to interrupt your routine in any way,' Lauren answered, and saw that sudden disconcerting gleam in the dark eyes again.

'What you really mean is that you'd prefer to be without my company, I think. Do you find me so undesirable a companion?'

'No,' she denied a little too hastily, 'of course not! I just don't want to put you to any trouble, that's all.'

'No trouble,' he assured her. 'Family comes before work.'

'I'm not family,' she said. 'Not really.'

'You bear the name of Quiros,' he pointed out on a crisper note. 'Blood is not the only measure. As the mother of my brother's sons, you are and will remain family, whatever your feelings on the matter.'

'I didn't mean to imply any distaste,' she said swiftly. 'The name of Quiros is obviously well respected. What I don't want is for you to feel in any way obligated towards me. I may not have the means to keep the twins in the style you have in mind, but I'm more than capable of looking after my own interests.'

'Are you?' His voice had lost the edge, the line of his mouth softening in a way that set her pulses beating suddenly faster. 'I think perhaps you need to look long and hard at your prospects before making such a statement. Are jobs in England so easily gained that you could secure one at choice with no recent experience to offer?'

'There are jobs which don't necessarily require experience,' she responded, trying to think of one.

'With equally low financial return, perhaps so.' He paused, studied her with enigmatic expression for a moment, then shrugged and dismissed the subject. 'Come, we should make a start while the guests are still at breakfast.'

Pacing at his side as they traversed the corridor leading to the public part of the castle, Lauren was intensely aware of his closeness. He wasn't touching her in any way, yet she could feel his body heat, catch the faint scent of aftershave or cologne, or whatever it was that Spanish men of his calibre might use; sense the latent power in that lean, lithe build. Rafael Javierre de Quiros was too much of a man for any woman to remain indifferent towards. Like his brother before him, he set her senses alight. Only it was not quite the same, because he also aroused hostility, and that was something else she was going to have to learn to deal with.

The castle was both extensive in area and superb in its upkeep. Lauren lost all sense of direction and all count of time during a tour which left out only the guest bedrooms. There was even a tiny chapel on the premises, utilising a room from which led the steps down to the dungeons.

Lauren made no attempt to conceal her emotions when shown the bare rock cells contained behind iron-barred doors, imagining the poor wretches incarcerated down here for months or even years at a time. Death would surely have been preferable to such a fate.

Death would certainly have been preferable to the agony inflicted by the instruments of torture still preserved in the chamber adjoining. She could almost hear the anguished screams echoing from the cold stained walls. To keep such gruesome relics at all was totally unnecessary in her estimation. Such cruel and barbaric times were best forgotten.

'It represents a part of our history which should never be cast from mind,' declared Rafael, guessing her exact thoughts with an accuracy she found even more disturbing. 'Our guests appear to find the place fascinating.'

'I find it repulsive,' Lauren stated shortly. 'I hope César and Nicolás are never brought down here.'

'I doubt very much if they would understand the significance,' came the seemingly indifferent reply, 'but your objection is of course noted. I'm glad to find that you occasionally speak of them by individual name instead of the collective "twins". They should be treated as separate persons, not two of a kind.'

'I do regard them as individuals!' she retorted furiously, all the more incensed by the criticism because she recognised a certain validity. 'You might have noticed that they're dressed differently.'

'More for easy recognition, I think,' he said, unmoved by her anger. 'They're identical in looks.'

Lauren caught herself up before she could say the words trembling on her lips. 'Twins usually are,' she got out instead.

'Only where formed from the same cell. It's quite possible to have two children born at the same time who are quite different in appearance.'

'I don't need any lessons in genetics, thanks,' she shot back at him. 'And I'll refer to *my* children the way *I* want!'

'Even though you know I'm right?' The query was deceptively mild, the dark eyes revealing a glitter to match her own. 'I thought you capable of more mature behaviour.'

'Which just goes to show how wrong first impressions can be.' The gloom and depressing atmosphere of her surroundings were doing nothing to help Lauren regain her equilibrium. 'I don't think this visit is turning out to have been such a good idea. The Spanish and English obviously hold very different views.'

'In this instance,' he said, 'more by reason of gender than of nationality, I believe. You resent what you regard as my interference simply because I'm a man, yes?'

'I resent your assumption that you have the right to interfere at all.' She said it between her teeth. 'If that's going to be the price of accepting help with education et cetera, then I don't think I'll bother. They're *my* sons, not yours!'

'If they were my sons, you would be my wife,' came the taut response. 'In which case you would have learned respect. Francisco obviously neglected his duty in more than the one aspect.' He gave her no time to form a reply. 'They're a part of him too, and in his absence are my responsibility by proxy. I have no intention of relinquishing that responsibility.'

The gloom of the chamber seemed to Lauren to have increased. Standing there, tall and dark and unsmiling, Rafael seemed as threatening as any past inquisitor. She wanted suddenly to run from him, to snatch up her sons and escape from this man, this place, this country, while she still could. It had been a mistake to come here at all; she knew that now.

'I think we'll have to agree to differ,' she said thickly. 'I can't be like your women.'

'You have no concept of the ways of our womenfolk,' he responded. 'Nor understanding of the male in any sphere, I think.' His tone was different, not exactly warm, but lacking the biting edge of a moment ago. 'We'll begin again. This time with a little more tolerance on both sides.' He paused, gaze narrowed to her face. 'Agreed?'

The reply was dragged from her. 'Agreed.'

'Good.' He made an abrupt movement. 'Then we'll go and drink coffee and discuss matters in surroundings more conducive than these.'

Which wouldn't be difficult to find, Lauren reflected wryly. This would be the very last time she ventured down here for certain. The whole place gave her the shivers.

There were a couple of guests looking round the little chapel when they emerged from the dungeon stairs. Judging from those already seen during the tour of the castle, Americans seemed to be in the majority among the present contingent.

'We don't have anything like this back home,' declared the beautifully dressed and coiffured woman. 'The whole place is unreal!'

'My ancestors lived very real lives,' Rafael assured her drily. 'We do, however, have a family ghost.'

'You do?' Her eyes lit up. 'Are we likely to see it?'

'Perhaps. He walks the battlements at night when the moon is full.'

'We missed it by a couple of weeks, then,' said the woman's husband, obviously not taking the story too seriously. 'A real shame. Are those the dungeons down there? Those folks we know who stayed here last year said to be sure to see them.'

'Then you must certainly do so,' Rafael answered. 'The lighting is poor, so you must watch your step.'

Lauren waited until the pair had disappeared down the winding staircase before voicing an opinion. 'Aren't you afraid of facing a massive lawsuit if they fall and injure themselves?'

The shrug was brief and dismissive. 'We're not in America. Would you prefer to take coffee outdoors or indoors?'

'Out, please,' she said, suddenly longing for the warmth of the sun. 'I should go and check on the boys first, though.'

'They're in good hands,' he stated flatly. 'How can they be expected to achieve the independence necessary to their future welfare if you're constantly with them?'

'They're four years old,' she returned, 'not fourteen!'

'But no longer infants at the breast.' He watched the colour come up in her cheeks with derision in the line of his mouth. 'You find the allusion distasteful?'

'I find your whole attitude degrading,' she parried with an effort.

'That was not the intention. I have your welfare at heart too. You have a life of your own to live, Lauren. Not just as a mother but as a woman, with a woman's needs.'

His voice had softened again in that disconcerting, heart-vibrating manner of his. She found herself transfixed by the dark eyes, stomach muscles contracting.

'I don't need you to tell me how I should live my life,' she said huskily. 'I'll do as I think fit. Right now, I'd like to see how my sons are getting on.'

Rafael made no immediate answer, just continued to study her with that same narrowed intensity. When he did speak his tone was unexpectedly mild. 'As you prefer.'

They found boys and nurse playing a form of quoits in a small grassed courtyard. Neither César nor Nicolás appeared to have missed her at all, Lauren was bound to acknowledge, and she tried without success to stifle the pang. Rafael was probably right in that too much of her life revolved around the twins. She had to learn to loosen up.

'I think I'd like that coffee now,' she said on a subdued note after watching the game for a few minutes. 'They're obviously doing fine.'

There was no element of 'I told you so' in the glance Rafael gave her. He wouldn't, she thought, waste his time on such petty emotions. A man of strong opinions and even stronger will, but one whose basic integrity was in no doubt.

'We'll have it served here,' he said, indicating a cast-iron bench seat set against the near wall. 'Sit there in the sun while I go and arrange it.'

Lauren did so, watching him go back indoors again with a dawning suspicion that this was where he had intended bringing her in the first place. Nicolás broke away from his game to come over to where she sat, his eyes shining with health and high spirits.

'We like it here, Mummy,' he announced, speaking collectively as always. 'Are you having a good time too?'

'Of course,' she assured him. 'I'm having a lovely time!'

Hypocrite! she told herself as the child scampered back to join his brother. Only what else could she have said on the face of it? Perhaps if she tried a little harder to get along with Rafael, she would start to find some enjoyment in this holiday after all.

Wheeled out on a trolley, the coffee arrived before he returned. There was also a jug of orange juice for the children. Elena accepted the cup Lauren poured for her without demur, but smilingly declined to take the seat also proffered, sitting down instead on the grass with the boys some distance away.

In her simple cotton dress, with her black hair rippling down her back and her face free of make-up, she looked no more than sixteen. Her parents and brother, Rafael had said, were also in his employment. No doubt, Lauren reflected, jobs here at the castle carried a certain prestige.

'I must apologise for leaving you so long,' he said when he did return some minutes later. 'There was a telephone call I had to make.'

'If you have business to attend to, I'll be perfectly all right on my own,' she assured him.

'The matter is taken care of,' he returned easily. 'We have yet to take a walk along the battlements. From there you can see everything there is to be seen.'

Including a long drop, she thought with an inward shudder. The sensible thing would be to admit to her acrophobia, of course, but she couldn't bring herself to say it. Only those who suffered the same symptoms could be relied upon to appreciate the fear.

With their juice finished, the children returned to their game. César in particular was proving to have a very good eye for distance, ringing the stake on several throws. Nicolás showed no concern over his brother's superior performance. Jealousy was an emotion unknown between the two. Eventually, Lauren knew, they would become bored with the game and start seeking further challenge, but for the present they seemed content. Happy, certainly, to be left in Elena's charge again.

Rafael took her up to the top of the keep via the same spiral staircase leading to her own room, bypassing both her floor and the next to emerge eventually on to a stone square not nearly large enough to afford Lauren any real sense of security. She felt the familiar tingling sensation in her ankles as she stood there gazing out through the battlements at the magnificent vista, the mounting terror at the very thought of moving away from the central block.

'It's possible to see Ronda itself from this side,' said Rafael, crossing over. 'Come, take a look.'

Somehow, she forced her legs to move, to carry her forward until she stood at his side before an embrasure that afforded a bare two feet of protection from the dizzying emptiness beyond. She was going to fall! she thought desperately. She could feel the trembling weakness spreading up through her knees, hear the buzzing in her ears.

She must have made some sound, for Rafael turned his head to look at her, taking in her white face and rigid jaw with instant comprehension. His arm came around her to draw her back from the parapet to the comparative safety of the central block again, holding her close until the trembling began to abate.

'Why did you not tell me how you felt about heights?' he grated in her ear. 'Why did you allow me to bring you up here?'

'I don't know,' she whispered shakily. 'It was silly of me, I suppose.'

'Foolish to the point of stupidity. There's no shame in acknowledging such a frailty. A matter of balance, no more.'

Her balance, Lauren thought, was disrupted in more ways than the one at the moment. She was intensely aware of the hard muscularity of his body, of the warmth and security of the arms curving her back. Her face was on a level with his throat, bared by the open collar of his shirt. She knew a sudden and almost irresistible urge to put her lips to the smooth olive skin—to know the taste of him, the smell of him. Francisco had been dead only three months, but it was more than two years since he had touched her. Not that she had wanted him to make love to her, knowing by then how many other women there had been, but her body still craved the fulfilment denied it.

'I'll be all right now,' she said shakily. 'I'm not going to pass out, or anything.'

Rafael drew back his head to look into her face, eyes black as night and twice as impenetrable. 'You feel capable of descending the steps?'

'If you go first,' she said. 'I'm sorry to be such a nuisance.'

Something sparked in his eyes for a fleeting moment as he looked at her, shortening her breath and causing her limbs to tremor anew, then he released her. 'Keep close at my back until we reach the lower floor,' he instructed. 'Hands on my shoulders as we descend.'

The steps were steep and narrow at this point, the spiral tight. Lauren was sure she would never have made it down again on her own without tumbling head first. The broad shoulders felt steady as rocks beneath her hands. Reaching the floor below, she drew a breath of pure relief. From here, as from her own floor, the steps were both wider and shallower, with handrails to grasp. She could negotiate those without difficulty.

Rafael made no attempt to continue on down, however, but drew her instead into a small but comfortably furnished *salón*, and bade her take a seat.

'We'll rest here for a moment or two,' he said, 'until you're fully recovered. A little brandy, perhaps?'

Lauren shook her head. 'I'm fine, really. The dizziness doesn't last. Is this your private *salón*?'

'Yes,' he acknowledged. 'I retreat here when I wish to be alone. Solitude renews the spirit.'

'I shouldn't have thought yours was ever low enough to need renewal,' she said, and saw his brow lift.

'You read me so well?'

'No.' She gave a wry little shrug. 'Just that you seem so totally in control of your life.'

'None of us can be totally in control,' he returned. 'Life holds many surprises.'

He hadn't taken a seat himself. Lauren wished that he would. Standing there, hands thrust into trouser pockets, he seemed to tower over her. She could still feel the pressure of his chest against her breasts—recall the way her nipples had tingled and peaked to the contact. They were doing so again at the very memory.

'Not always pleasant ones,' she agreed, hoping that nothing of what she was thinking showed in her face. It was shameful to be having these feelings at all for a man she scarcely knew. Francisco's own brother, for heaven's sake! 'It must be getting close to lunchtime,' she added a little desperately. 'I'll need to tidy myself up.'

'We normally eat our meal at two o'clock,' Rafael advised, 'but if you're hungry now I'll arrange for food to be brought.'

It was, Lauren realised, glancing at her watch, only just gone twelve. Hunger was the last thing on her mind—for food, at any rate.

'My body clock is way out,' she said with an attempt at humour. 'I can wait, thanks. All the same, I'd like to tidy myself up.' She came to her feet as she spoke, unsurprised to feel the unsteadiness still in her legs. Fear of a different kind this time, and one Rafael must not be allowed to guess. 'It was good of you to spend so long with me, when I know how busy you must be.'

'The day,' he said, 'is not yet over. We're to visit Ronda this afternoon.'

'Are you sure you have the time?'

'Time,' he said, 'is the servant, not the master. We must use it to our advantage. Take care descending the steps.'

It wasn't the steps she had to worry about, Lauren thought wryly, making her escape, so much as her own wayward emotions. From now on she must steer well clear of any physical contact at all with her brother-in-law.

CHAPTER THREE

THE twins were full of their morning. Already they had picked up one or two Spanish words, Lauren noted, listening to their breathless account. She hoped Elena wasn't counting on a break this afternoon; it had been a long time since either of them had taken an afternoon nap.

They had stayed remarkably clean for once. Apart from a quick wash of face and hands, and the use of a hairbrush, they needed no further sprucing up for lunch. With the outing to Ronda in mind, Lauren exchanged her flowered cotton skirt and blouse for a pale blue dress, livening it up with some amber beads and holding back her hair from her face with a narrow bandeau the same colour. Francisco had considered her taste in clothes far too conservative. He had probably been right too, only miniskirts just weren't her thing. She doubted if they were to Rafael's taste either.

Lunch was a leisurely meal. Too leisurely for the twins, who found sitting still for even ten minutes a strain. Rafael had Elena come and take the pair of them out in the end, with instructions that they were to spend an hour resting.

'I doubt if they're going to sleep at all,' said Lauren when they were gone from the room.

'I said rest,' Rafael pointed out. 'At their age, they have need of a quiet recuperative period. Elena will see that they stay in their room.'

She wouldn't, Lauren thought, like to take a bet on it! His peremptory assumption of authority rankled more than a little, even though she could see the sense in what he was saying. Given half a chance, he would have them all jumping through hoops to his command!

'If you have something to say to me, then say it,' he invited, watching her expression. 'You consider it not my place to organise their day?'

'It's your house,' she prevaricated. 'Castle, I mean. I can't blame you for not wanting them running all over the place.'

'They need order in their lives,' he declared. 'I have a feeling that you tend to take the easier option.'

It was too close to the truth for comfort. Lauren could feel herself flushing. 'It's so easy for the uninitiated to criticise!' she snapped back.

'Meaning that, as a childless bachelor, I'm in no position to judge?' There was more than a hint of mockery in the dark eyes. 'Perhaps not. But can you honestly say that I'm wrong?'

She bit her lip, aware of being backed into a corner. 'It isn't all that easy dealing with two at the same time.'

'Especially where the father takes little part. Did Francisco have no feeling at all for his sons?'

'He didn't pay them all that much attention,' Lauren admitted, and immediately felt disloyal. 'But I'm sure he loved them in his own way.'

Rafael shook his head. 'You've no cause to defend my brother. His behaviour was inexcusable.'

'He's dead,' she said with deliberation. 'I'd prefer to let him rest in peace.'

The dark head inclined. 'You're more forgiving than I would be in your place, but I respect the sentiment.'

His tone altered. 'Tell me, have you had the boys assessed?'

'If you mean with regard to intelligence level, then yes,' she acknowledged.

'And the results?'

'They both have extra-high IQs.' Lauren strove to keep her voice matter-of-fact. 'The important thing, I'm told, is not to treat them as anything special—to let them progress at their own pace.'

'Very wise advice,' Rafael agreed. 'They need to experience all the delights of childhood.'

Something in his tone made her regard him with sudden insight. 'You had the same problem yourself?'

'You see advanced intelligence as a problem?'

'In some respects. I worry about how they'll cope in school if they have to keep pace with their actual age-group.'

'Badly,' he said. 'Which is yet another reason why you have to accept help in the matter. There are schools equipped to deal with such children.'

'The kind you attended yourself?'

The firm mouth slanted briefly. 'My advancement was not as great. I'll begin enquiries at once.'

'We have until September,' Lauren pointed out, laying delicate stress on the 'we'. 'There's no immediate rush. I can gather some information myself once I'm back home.'

Something flickered in his eyes, then he shrugged. 'Of course. And in the meantime we must see that you enjoy your stay. You are ready to leave for Ronda?'

As ready, Lauren reflected, as she would ever be. Going anywhere at all on her own with this man was likely to prove a mistake, but, short of admitting that he disturbed her too much for comfort, there was no way out of it.

They took the white coupé for the drive into the town. Dressed now in close-fitting green shirt and equally close-fitting white trousers, Rafael looked darker-skinned than ever. The loosely rolled sleeves revealed muscular fore-arms lightly covered in hair bleached by the sun to several shades lighter than that on his head. His wrists were sinewy, the hands holding the wheel long and fleshless, fingers tapering. Sensitive, Lauren thought, and felt a tremor run through her. This had to stop, she told herself desperately. No good could come of it.

He drove right through the modern section to park the car in the Plaza de España. A couple of coaches were off-loading tourists armed with the inevitable cameras. A cross unfortunately necessary to the prosperity of the area, Rafael returned drily when Lauren commented on the general ruination of peace and tranquillity.

'It gets much worse than this in the summer months,' he said. 'The traffic is nose to tail across the bridge, with accidents a frequent occurrence. The coaches alone are a hazard. It would be better if tourists were banned from driving into the town at all, but few of them know how to walk very far. I suggest we visit the bull-ring to begin with,' he added. 'The oldest ring in the whole of Spain. Pedro Romero himself fought here.' He registered her expression with a quizzical lift of a brow. 'You disapprove of the bull-fight?'

'I disapprove of any form of cruelty to animals,' Lauren acknowledged. 'And I don't much care whose toes I tread on in saying it!'

The smile was tolerant. 'That I can believe. However, there's no *corrida* scheduled today, so you may rest easy and enjoy the architecture alone. I think you'll find it worthy of study.'

It would be labouring the point to refuse on principle, Lauren decided. Viewing the premises was hardly akin to condoning the practice. Bull-fighting wasn't going to be eradicated by loud-mouthed foreigners calling the odds. It would take a total change of national attitude, and that was unlikely, to say the least.

Only a step or two away from where they had parked, the Plaza de Toros was entered via a huge ornate doorway. The two coachloads of tourists had begun their sightseeing on the bridge itself, and at present there were few other people inside.

Lauren was struck by the sheer size of the ring. Standing in the middle of it, gazing up at the circling tiers of seats rising beneath double sets of finely wrought arches, she had to acknowledge the picturesque quality of the scene. The sheer clarity of light gave added depth and vibrancy to the colours of sand and stone and red-painted woodwork.

A door on the far side gave access to the museum. Lauren turned a blind eye on the many posters and photographs depicting various famous matadors in action, concentrating instead on the items of apparel displayed. The capes in particular were works of art in themselves, each one intricately embroidered in silk thread by hand, each design different.

'They're beautiful!' she declared. 'Workmanship like that has to be admired.'

'Even for such a purpose?' Rafael shook his head as she opened her mouth to reply. 'No, we'll leave it right there. Our viewpoints differ. That we must both accept.'

And not only where bull-fighting was concerned, she reflected. They were at odds on most subjects, it seemed.

From the bull-ring they traversed a traffic-free street lined both sides with shops and stalls. Either siesta was over, or the traders in general followed Rafael's example in ignoring it, as business appeared to be going on apace. Judging from the numbers of non-nationals thronging the street, more coaches had arrived. Lauren was thankful to turn off into the quieter back streets.

'I hadn't anticipated so many this early in the year,' Rafael admitted. 'Next time we'll make it an evening visit when the coaches have departed.'

'You don't have to feel under any obligation to entertain me while I'm here,' Lauren protested. 'You must have work to do.'

'Nothing beyond Gabriel's ability to take care of, for the next few days at least,' came the smooth reply. 'Tonight we have guests at dinner, all of them eager to meet you.'

Curious would be more like it, she thought, stifling her trepidation. It stood to reason that the sudden appearance of Francisco's wife and children would give rise to speculation. No doubt many would believe her an opportunist, here only for what she could get from the family coffers. It shouldn't matter what people she neither knew nor cared about thought, but it did.

They arrived back at the Plaza de España to find two of the coaches on the point of departure and few other tourists in immediate evidence.

'Now, while it is quiet, would be the best time to take a walk across the bridge and back,' suggested Rafael. 'The only way to deal with vertigo is to accustom oneself gradually to heights instead of trying to avoid them altogether.'

Which was true enough, Lauren knew. The bridge itself had been there for more than two hundred years;

it was hardly going to choose the very moment she set foot on it to collapse into the abyss.

'I'm sure you're right,' she said, trying to sound positive. 'It's high time I conquered it.'

All the same, the thought alone of all that empty space beneath caused her lower legs to tingle as they moved on to the bridge. Iron-railed embrasures set within the side-walls afforded dizzying glimpses of the gorge, drawing her eyes despite every effort not to look. Rafael put a steadying hand under her elbow, causing a tingle of a different nature, and brought her to a halt at the central viewpoint.

'Stand here for a moment or two and look at the view beyond rather than below,' he bid her.

Standing right behind her, he rested both hands on her waist, holding her firmly. She could feel his breath on her hair, his body heat at her back. Vertigo became secondary to other, more imperative responses. She had to forcibly stop herself from leaning into him.

'I'm all right,' she got out. 'Really, I am!'

'I can feel the tension in you,' he said softly. 'In a moment or two, as your senses adjust, it will begin to lessen.'

Not while he continued to hold her, it wouldn't, Lauren knew. She doubted that he was unaware of her response to his touch. It probably amused him to know how he affected her.

'Your waist is so small,' he murmured. 'I can almost span it between my hands. One would never guess that you had borne even one child, much less two!'

'I suppose I'm just naturally thin,' she countered, and sensed his smile.

'The word suggests shapelessness, and you're far from that.'

Her heart was thudding against her ribcage, her every sense alive to the sheer seductive quality of his tone. It meant nothing, she told herself with emphasis. She was his brother's wife; his interest in her went no deeper than that. She just wasn't used to compliments. These last two years, Francisco had treated her more like a piece of furniture than an attractive woman.

'I'm all right now,' she said abruptly. 'You don't need to hold me any longer. The railing is safeguard enough.'

She made herself move on as he dropped his hands, more afraid of being touched again than she was of falling. Feeling this way over a man she didn't even like very much was not only wrong, it was disgusting! He was her brother-in-law, for heaven's sake!

They made the return journey without pause. There was an enigmatic little smile on Rafael's lips as he put her into the car. Lauren was beginning to wish she'd never come to Spain at all. At least back home she had felt in charge of things. Here, she felt anything but.

'These people who are coming to dinner,' she said on the way back to the castle, 'did they know Francisco?'

'Not all,' Rafael answered. 'The Caldases are relatively new to the area. Isabella is close to your own age, and also a mother. You and she should have much in common.'

Lauren doubted it. Their lifestyles alone must be poles apart. She wasn't looking forward to this evening. Keeping her eyes open into the early hours would be difficult enough. Dreadful if she fell asleep at table!

'I hope some of them speak English,' she said.

'All of them,' came the dry reply. 'The English themselves are the ones most reluctant to learn other languages. You should take the opportunity to study Spanish.'

'I'm hardly going to be here long enough to have need,' she pointed out.

There was no answer to that, just a somewhat disquieting firming of lip and jawline. Lauren tried to ignore the sudden uneasiness. No matter how he might feel about his brother's sons, England was still their homeland, and hers the choice to remain there. Nothing was going to change that.

Gabriel was just getting out of his own car when they drew into the courtyard. He looked disgruntled to see the two of them together.

'I followed every instruction,' he said in answer to Rafael's query. 'There are no immediate problems.'

'In which case, we may both of us relax for a time and enjoy our visitors,' replied his brother smoothly. 'I arranged a small dinner party for this evening, in order to introduce Lauren to our friends and neighbours. Alicia will, of course, accompany her parents.'

Gabriel's expression underwent an abrupt change. When he spoke it was in his own language, a short sharp phrase which narrowed Rafael's eyes and drew an equally short and sharp response. Gabriel shook his head and turned away.

A difference of opinion over suitable liaisons, perhaps, Lauren guessed, with a hazy idea of how such matters were handled over here. Betrothal as children wasn't uncommon, even in this day and age, she believed.

'I'll go and see what the boys are up to,' she said hastily, and left the two of them to it.

She found the twins with Elena in the library. They were all three of them browsing through a set of encyclopaedias, with Elena translating as they went. Greeted quite casually by her sons, who were obviously too interested in what they were doing to break off, Lauren felt like an interloper. She had to forcibly remind herself that a clinging mother demanding constant reassurance of her importance in their lives was the last thing they needed—the last thing she wanted to become. She had, after all, been away from them only a matter of a few brief hours.

It was Elena herself who declared the reading session over with a firmness accepted, if not too willingly, by both boys.

'They are so advanced for their age,' she declared as she returned the volume to its place. 'Already they are learning to speak our language.'

'*Sí*!' chorused the two of them promptly, then broke into reassuringly childish giggles.

'*Buenos días*,' said Rafael from the doorway, and they both looked round.

'*Tardes*,' corrected Nicolás. 'It's afternoon now.'

'So it is.' Rafael kept his tone quite level. 'Almost time for supper, in fact.'

Elena looked a little anxious. 'I hope I do no wrong in teaching the Spanish?'

'Of course not,' Lauren assured her, and added lightly, 'They'll be able to impress all their friends with it when they get back home.'

'We don't want to go home,' chimed in César. 'We like it best here.'

Lauren's heart gave a painful jerk. 'We're only here on holiday,' she declared. 'Just for two weeks.'

'There's no limitation on my part,' put in Rafael smoothly. 'You're welcome to make your home here at Callahora. We should discuss the matter.'

Lauren stared at him nonplussed, aware of conflicting emotions. They had been here in Spain little more than twenty-four hours. Hardly long enough for any such matter to even be mooted, much less decided upon. It was no spur-of-the-moment suggestion, she suspected. Rafael was far from the type to make such an offer without having given the subject careful consideration. It was out of the question, of course.

'It's more than kind of you,' she said, 'but quite unnecessary. Our home might not be on a par with all this, but it is home.'

'Now is not the time to talk it through,' Rafael answered firmly. 'I have some matters to take care of, if you will excuse me for the moment.'

There was little else Lauren could do but withdraw along with Elena and the twins and leave him to it. César hadn't meant what he said, she assured herself. The castle was a novelty, that was all; the kind of place most children would find fascinating. Once they were back home they would soon forget. In the meantime, she had some straightening out to do with Rafael.

With dinner more than four hours away she joined the boys for a light supper, glad to relieve Elena of her supervision for the day. She was going to need to watch herself for possessiveness, she thought wryly. Seeing them off to nursery school three mornings a week this last year had been bad enough; losing them for the whole day was going to be infinitely worse.

A job would not only provide extra income but occupy her mind at the same time. Always providing she could find one, of course. As Rafael had so rightly pointed out, she had little experience in any sphere except child-rearing to offer.

So how about child-minding on a self-employed basis? came the thought. According to reports, good reliable ones were at a premium. On the other hand, was she basically fond enough of children *en masse* to take charge of other peoples' offspring? Patience and tolerance didn't come all that high on her list of virtues—short as it was to begin with.

She was going around in circles and getting nowhere very fast, she decided. There was a whole summer to go before it became necessary to make any such choices.

Accustomed to going to bed while it was still light, the twins put up no more than their usual objections at seven. Lauren's hopes that the extra stimulation would have tired them to the point of immediate sleepiness proved fruitless. After three stories, they were still wide awake and asking for more. At home, she would have left them in their room to follow their own devices until sleep finally claimed them, but she didn't feel able to risk that here. In no circumstances would she lock them in either. That smacked too much of forced confinement.

The three of them finished up playing a word game she had brought with her until exhaustion finally overcame the pair. Tucking them in, kissing each smooth forehead, Lauren was swamped by love. She was their mother. Nothing or no one could take that away from her. She might have to learn to loosen it, but the bond would always be there.

It was already gone nine o'clock, she was dismayed to find on reaching her own room. Rafael had said they would be taking pre-dinner drinks in the *salón*, which meant she would probably be expected down there by half-past nine at the latest. Up to now, she hadn't even given a thought to what she was going to wear for the occasion. Something dressy, she supposed.

She settled on a plain black sheath of a dress with scooped neckline and long tight sleeves that she had bought three years ago for one of the few occasions when Francisco had taken her out. It still fitted well enough, she was glad to find on donning the garment, outlining her figure without clinging. The addition of a short string of pearls and matching ear studs completed the outfit. Her wedding present from Francisco, and the only items of good jewellery she possessed. There had been happy times in the beginning before he had been turned off by her altering shape. Some men might find their pregnant wives attractive still, but Francisco hadn't been one of them.

Lauren thrust the memories aside determinedly. It was all in the past, and should be left there. If she ever married again, it would be to a man who loved her for what she was rather than just the way she looked. *If* she ever married again. Right now, she felt it unlikely she would ever want to.

Wearing plain black suede shoes, and carrying a small suede bag, she made her way down to the lower floor on the stroke of the half-hour. The sound of voices came from the *salón*. Taking a deep breath, and summoning a smile that felt stiff as a board, Lauren pushed open the door and went in.

At first glance the room seemed to be full of people. Devastating in a cream tuxedo, Rafael detached himself from the group to come across and take her by the arm with a smile that tugged at her stomach muscles.

'You look very beautiful,' he murmured, filling her with a sudden new confidence and the ability to smile right back.

'Thank you,' she said equally softly. 'You look very handsome yourself.'

Dark eyes took on a gleam, whether of derision or gratification she couldn't be sure. More probably the former, she thought. Rafael was hardly the type to accept flattery at face value.

There were, she saw as he drew her forward, no more than eight or nine other people in the room. Gabriel was seated beside a young woman whom Lauren took to be the aforementioned Alicia. His set expression lightened as he caught her eyes—a change not unnoted by his companion, whose face revealed sudden dejection.

For the next few moments Lauren was immersed in introductions. Julio de Caldas was around Rafael's age, his wife Isabella several years younger. A good-looking couple, friendly without being over-effusive in their greeting, unlike the Floreses who were, it appeared, Alicia's parents. Alicia herself was around twenty years of age, Lauren judged, with a scraped-back hairstyle that did nothing at all to enhance her looks, and wearing a dress that her mother must have chosen. The big dark eyes lacked sparkle.

The eyes of the woman next to be introduced held an unmistakable and disconcerting animosity. In her mid to late twenties, Nina Ortega was possessed of a beauty Lauren found off-putting in its very lack of even the slightest imperfection, every feature chiselled from marble. Her skin was smooth as olive silk, her hair a gleaming black coil, her body, in its scarlet gown, statuesque. Beside her, Lauren felt she paled into insignificance. She kept her smile going with an effort as she acknowledged the other's cool greeting.

Her companion was of a different stamp altogether. Xaviour Ríos exuded charm from every pore. Not to be trusted an inch despite it, was Lauren's judgement as he raised the back of her hand to his lips in an extravagant gesture that brought an added glitter to Nina's eyes. No man should look upon a woman with such obvious admiration when already accompanied by another.

Rafael didn't much like it either, if she were to judge from the tension in the arm touching hers. His displeasure would be for Nina's sake rather than her own, she was sure. There had been something in the way in which he said the woman's name that suggested some degree of intimacy—a thought which brought a deep-down pang. No concern of hers, she told herself stoutly, and knew that she lied.

The gin and tonic she had asked for in hand, she found herself gravitating quite naturally towards Isabella.

'I understand you have a child too?' she said.

'A daughter,' the other confirmed. 'Three years of age. We would very much like a son, but it has yet to happen for us. You must be so proud to have two sons!'

'I am,' Lauren confirmed. 'Although I wouldn't have minded girls either.' She laughed. 'I suppose a girl *and* a boy would have been the absolute ideal. Not that I'd be prepared to exchange either Nicolás or César now, of course.'

'Such good Spanish names,' approved Julio. 'Francisco's choice or your own?'

'A joint agreement,' Lauren replied levelly, with no intention of relating the truth of the matter. César had been acceptable enough, if a little over-fancy for her tastes, but Nicolás would have been named Felix had Francisco had his way, and that she had been unable to stomach. A compromise had been effected in the end, but he had never really forgiven her for disputing his right to name his own sons. Yet another nail in the coffin of their marriage.

'Does the name of Javierre de Quiros command the same respect in your country?' asked Isabella curiously.

'As a matter of fact,' Lauren confessed, 'Francisco dropped the Javierre some time ago. He found it too much trouble when it came to filling in forms.'

'Is that so?' said Rafael on a hardened note, joining the three of them with a refill of Julio's glass. 'I trust you'll allow Nicolás and César their full title?'

'Of course,' she assured him, adding with some deliberation, 'If that's what they want when they're old enough to decide. The Quiros itself is enough to set them apart.'

'Only in England,' he said flatly. 'Here, in Spain, they would be with their own kind.'

'They're only half Spanish,' she returned, concealing her anger at this untimely renewal of what should surely be a private argument.

'But they look wholly so,' came the smooth rejoinder. 'The image of their father,' he added to the Caldases. 'One would never know there was English blood in their veins!'

'Until you heard them speak.' Lauren was doing her best to hang on to her temper. Rafael had no right to do this to her! She forced a light note. 'Perhaps my colouring would have come through in a daughter.'

'Your beauty too,' said Julio gallantly. 'Colouring such as yours is not unknown in Spain, although it is far from common. Should you stay here and marry again, you may well found a whole new genetic line!'

'An unlikely event,' Lauren smiled, 'but thank you for the compliment, anyway.'

'You do not care for our country?' he asked.

'I haven't seen very much of it,' she was bound to admit.

'Then Rafael must lose no time in showing you.'

'That,' said the man in question, 'is my intention. I think it time we took our places for dinner.'

Today was Friday, Lauren reflected, stifling the sharp retort she had been about to make. Before the weekend was out she would either have convinced this despotic brother-in-law or hers that he was wasting his time, or she would be on her way home with the twins in tow. What she would *not* be doing was arguing the toss for the next two weeks!

Finding herself placed in the hostess's position at the opposite end of the dining table from Rafael himself was a confirmation of a planned objective on his part. He had intended all along that his brother's sons should remain with him. As their mother, she had to be included too, of course, although he would no doubt have preferred sole possession.

Now was hardly the time to call him out, she thought, gritting her teeth as she took her seat. Later, after everyone had left—no matter what hour it was—she would make it finally and irrevocably clear to him that there was no chance. If he refused to accept that then the three of them would leave first thing in the morning.

With Señor Flores on one hand, and Julio on the other, she had little opportunity for introspection over the following three hours or so. Course after course came and went, wine was drunk and conversation flowed.

Occasionally, Lauren found her glance caught and held by the woman seated next to Gabriel, and made every effort not to respond to the enmity she saw there. That it was her very presence the other resented was more than obvious, yet if there was something going on between her and Rafael, what was she doing here with another man in tow? Anyway, she had no cause for jealousy. Rafael had no designs other than to secure the future of his nephews.

Francisco's name was hardly mentioned. It was apparent that everyone here knew of his disgrace, and found the memory discomfiting. Lauren found it so herself. A girl had died, and Francisco had been responsible.

Deny it though she had to Rafael, he had made an attempt to persuade her into an abortion too, but her impassioned refusal had convinced him. She had been as surprised as anyone when he settled for marriage instead. In many ways, came the wry thought, she might have been happier left on her own. Single parents might find life a struggle, but at least they were spared the heartbreak of a meaningless relationship.

Coffee and liqueurs were taken in the *salón* around one o'clock. Apart from herself, no one was showing any sign of fatigue, thought Lauren, fighting to keep her eyes open. General conversation was conducted in English for her benefit, with only the occasional foray into Spanish between individuals. Nina made no attempt to speak to her at all.

No great loss, Lauren told herself. If Rafael was, or had been, involved with the woman, it said little for his judgement.

Catching his glance on her, she gave him a hard-eyed stare, refusing to be the first to turn away. She saw one brow lift in challenge, and knew she was in for a fight. Rather than setting her on edge, the knowledge served to put her on her mettle. Accustomed as he might be to ruling the roost, he was going to find her a tough hen to control!

CHAPTER FOUR

THE party finally broke up at two o'clock. Wide awake now, and geared for action, Lauren found it difficult to stay outwardly calm and collected as farewells were made.

'Rafael must bring you to our home,' said Isabella. 'Perhaps on Sunday when the children can play together?'

'I'll look forward to it,' Lauren replied, not about to intimate that she might not even be here by then.

Saying goodnight to Nina was like being run over by an ice truck. The woman made no attempt whatsoever to conceal her feelings. Rafael seemed unaware of it; either that, or he was deliberately turning a blind eye. The reason she was here at all was still something of a puzzle. She was hardly the type to settle for the hand of friendship after a closer relationship had died a death.

The Floreses were last to leave. Standing with Lauren in the doorway while Rafael saw the trio to their car, Gabriel gave vent to a sigh.

'I can never,' he declared, 'marry Alicia! She means nothing to me!'

'No one can force you,' Lauren responded mildly. 'Surely all you have to do is say no?'

'I have,' he said. 'Time and time again!'

'To Alicia herself?'

'No.' He sounded suddenly deflated. 'I've no wish to marry her, but neither do I wish to shame her. The betrothal took place when we were children. We were not consulted. Alicia has always accepted that one day she would be my wife.'

'While you never did?'

He shrugged. 'I gave the matter little real thought until this last year when the pressure began to mount. Rafael believes me committed to the marriage.'

'That's an antediluvian attitude, if ever I heard one!' she said, and saw his brow wrinkle.

'What does that mean?'

'Before the ark.' She made some attempt to simplify the explanation. 'Childhood betrothals must be out of date, even here.'

'My father held faith with the old ways,' he said. 'As does Señor Flores still.'

'And Rafael too, it seems.' Her tone was caustic, drawing his gaze.

'You find my brother unpalatable?'

Lauren had to smile despite herself. 'I suppose that's one way of putting it.' She hesitated before adding, 'Did you know he intended our stay to be permanent?'

It was Gabriel's turn to hesitate. 'I expected some attempt to be made to convince you, yes,' he said at length. 'Francisco did wrong, but he's still a Quiros—as are his sons. Rafael would naturally wish to see them reared as such.'

'And you agree with that?'

'I would very much like you to stay with us,' he returned softly. 'You must know that already.'

Lauren bit her lip, aware of having left the door wide open. 'It's nice of you,' she said, 'and much appreciated, but you must see how impossible it would be. We have a home of our own.'

'But not one such as this. As Francisco's sons, Nicolás and César have a birthright. As his wife, you have rights too.'

'Among them being the entitlement to choose my own place of abode, wouldn't you say?' She shook her head at him as he hesitated again. 'I feel the same way about that as you do about being expected to marry Alicia. Surely you, of all people, can understand my viewpoint?'

The agreement came with reluctance. 'Yes, I understand. All the same, I wish you would stay.'

'I can't.' If the truth were only known, reflected Lauren wryly, she dared not even contemplate it. The effect Rafael had on her was too disturbing to be put aside. She would never in a thousand years be able to regard him as a brother.

He was coming back now after pressing the drawbridge control, tuxedo gleaming in the dim lighting of the courtyard. It was to be hoped that all hotel guests were safely tucked up in their beds by now, Lauren reflected, although it seemed more than likely considering the hour. She stood her ground as he came up, meeting the dark gaze with a carefully controlled expression.

'I think we have things to discuss,' she said.

'The hour is late,' he returned. 'The morning will be soon enough.'

'It's morning now.' She was determined not to be browbeaten into postponement.

Broad shoulders lifted briefly. 'Very well. We'll return to the *salón*.'

He proffered no invitation to Gabriel to accompany them, nor did the latter attempt to do so. Lauren girded her loins for the coming conversation, going over in her mind what she wanted to say. No beating about the bush, she decided, but straight in for the kill.

Heart beating fast and hard, she swung to face him the moment they were inside the room, steeling herself against the sheer impact of his regard.

'I'm going to say it once and once only,' she got out. 'There's no way that the twins and I are coming to live here in Spain. Either you accept that, or we're leaving right away!'

'And how exactly would you propose to pay for your tickets home?' came the smooth response. 'I doubt if you have funds enough of your own readily available to cover the cost.'

The wind taken momentarily from her sails, Lauren stared at him in confusion. 'I—— We'd use the return half of the ones you arranged for us, of course,' she said. 'I still have them.'

'They were cancelled this morning.' The statement was matter-of-fact.

She drew in a deep, steadying breath. 'Then you'd better make arrangements to reinstate them!'

'I think not.' His tone was level, his whole attitude composed. 'I already began proceedings to become the children's legal guardian. They won't be allowed to leave the country at all until the matter is resolved.'

She said thickly, 'That's impossible! They're English, not Spanish. You can't just take over! The law won't allow it!'

'They are my brother's sons, which makes them Spanish in my eyes,' came the unmoved response. 'And what would you know of Spanish law? They are here, and here they stay. Whether you stay with them is your own choice, of course. Naturally, I'd be prepared to cover your costs.'

Lauren could hardly believe this was happening. Ruthless, had been her recent summing-up of this man, but just how much so she hadn't even come close to realising.

'You really believe I'd go home without them?' she said, rallying her forces with an effort, and saw a faint smile cross the lean features.

'No, I don't believe that for a moment, but you had to be given the opportunity. You are more than welcome to make your home here at Callahora.'

'As what?' she demanded. 'Some kind of secondary parent?' She shook her head emphatically. 'They're *my* sons. You have no rights over them. The British authorities will soon sort this out!'

'You would have to return to England to begin such legislation,' Rafael pointed out.

'There's the British consul.'

'Who can do little in actuality except register a protest—even if you could reach the consulate. The nearest is in Málaga. You would find it a long walk.'

Lauren looked at him in stupefaction. 'You're saying we're prisoners here?'

The smile came again, satirical in its slant. 'I have no intention of utilising the dungeons, you may rest assured. Without transport, however, you are confined to the immediate area. You have no driving skills, I believe.'

It was more statement than question, and one she had no intention of disputing. She had learned to drive before meeting Francisco, and still held a valid licence. The way things were going, she might have need of it—although stealing a car would hardly solve the problem of getting back home to England.

'Does Gabriel know about this?' she asked.

'He knows of my interest in securing the future of our nephews, yes.'

'And he agrees with your methods?'

'I haven't discussed the matter with him.'

'Because you knew he wouldn't go along with it!'

The muscles around the firm mouth tightened. 'It matters little what Gabriel may or may not agree with. The decision was mine alone.'

'You can't rule everyone's life the way you rule your brother's!' Lauren shot back at him. 'You may live in a castle, but king you're not!'

'I am what I am,' he said. 'I make no apologies.'

'A tyrant,' she spat. 'I despise you!'

A new and infinitely more dangerous light sprang alive in the dark eyes as he studied her. When he spoke it was with softer inflexion. 'But that fails to stop you from wanting me—the same way that I want you.'

Her breath caught in her throat. For a long moment she could only gaze at him, too stunned to find words. 'You don't know what you're talking about,' she got out at length.

'I'm talking about this,' he said, and reached out a hand to pull her to him.

The kiss was soul-shaking. One hand behind her head, the other arm pinioning her against him, he held her without effort when she attempted to break away. She could feel the whole lean, hard length of him, the unremitting pressure on breast and thigh; the commanding yet somehow almost delicate persuasion of his lips. Her struggles gave way to a force more potent than self-preservation, softening her own lips in answer—petalling them open to the heady demand.

It was Rafael himself who broke the spell, although he made no immediate attempt to release her.

'You see,' he murmured. 'An emotion shared by both. I knew the moment I set eyes on you that I would have to have you, Lauren. It was written in the stars!'

'I'm your brother's wife.' Her voice seemed to be coming from a long, long way away. 'You can't...we can't...'

'We can do whatever we wish with our lives,' he declared. 'Be whatever we desire to be. Would you try to deny that you want me?'

A tremor ran the length of her spine. She stiffened in his arms, fighting to regain control of her senses. 'This is contemptible,' she whispered. 'Let go of me, Rafael!'

'Not until you give me an answer,' he said. 'A truthful answer.'

'All right!' The words were torn from her. 'So I want you. It's purely physical, and I hate myself for it. Now, will you let me go?'

There was a suspended moment when he made no move, then he dropped his arms, allowing her to draw back away from him. 'There will be other, more congruous times.'

'No, there won't.' She was swept by shame of what she had just revealed. 'I may not be able to control the way I feel but I can control the way I act. Even if you weren't attempting to steal my children from me, do you really think I'd enter into any kind of sexual liaison with my husband's brother?'

His regard was narrowed, the handsome features suddenly harder. 'You would have little choice if I chose to take you.'

Lauren curled a lip. 'You mean rape me, don't you?'

'It would be no rape,' he denied. 'Your response to me just now was far from reluctant.'

Her face flamed. 'The element of surprise, that's all. You wouldn't find me as weak again!'

'No?' The pause was deliberated. 'You would care to put that theory to the test?'

She drew back instinctively. 'I have more important things to think about,' she said thickly. 'Do you still intend going through with this plan of yours?'

'With regard to Nicolás and César?' The dark head inclined. 'But of course. Why would I have changed my mind?'

Why indeed? Lauren scarcely knew which way to turn. All very well to talk about it being beyond his power to do as he was threatening, but how did she know it was? Spanish law was outside her province; she wasn't all that conversant with English law, if it came to that. In a case such as this, possession might very well prove the ruling factor in the end. It had in other instances of child abduction she had read about. The fact that Rafael was only the twins' uncle rather than their father might make little difference in these particular circumstances. Certainly, he could provide them with a far better standard of living than she could herself.

Regardless, she wasn't going simply to sit back and accept his jurisdiction, she told herself fiercely. She would fight him tooth and nail!

'I'm going to bed,' she said with control. 'Hopefully, you'll have seen sense by morning.'

'So, I trust, will you,' he returned. 'You have much to gain from compliance, Lauren, nothing at all from resistance—in any sphere.'

'Meaning I hand over my sons *and* my body?' She shook her head. 'You'll get neither on a platter!'

His lips twitched. 'I ask for no trimmings. By all means sleep on the matter.' He stood aside to allow her free access to the door. 'We'll talk again later when you have had the time and opportunity to consider the advantages.'

'Of becoming your concubine?' Her tone was scathing. 'I'd as soon enter a convent!'

Some indecipherable expression flickered briefly across the hard-boned face. 'Then perhaps you should become my wife instead.'

How long Lauren just stood there gaping at him she couldn't afterwards have said. Tall, lean and enigmatic, he made no move towards her but simply waited impassively for her reply. When she did find her voice it sounded totally unlike her own.

'I don't find that in the least bit amusing!'

Dark brows lifted. 'It was hardly meant to amuse. On the contrary, it would solve all our problems.'

'And create a whole lot more!' She still couldn't accept that he was serious. 'I'm your sister-in-law, for heaven's sake!'

'A relationship bearing no blood tie, and therefore of no consequence,' he rejoined. 'Nicolás and César have need of a father. Better one with family feeling for them than some stranger.'

'What makes you so sure I'd consider remarrying at all?' she countered, playing for time in which to sort out her churning thoughts.

'Because not to do so would deprive your sons of a relationship essential to their development. Single-parent families may be the fashion in your country, but here the interests of the child come first. Boys, especially, have need of masculine influence in their home lives.'

'You mean discipline, don't you?' she said tautly. 'Spare the rod and spoil the child!'

'Discipline isn't necessarily synonymous with chastisement,' Rafael denied. 'Children need the security of a well ordered structure. Given your inclination towards indulgence, together with their advanced intelligence, they could soon become out of control. Francisco neglected to lay the groundwork in their early years, but it isn't too late.'

'Have you any idea how utterly pompous you sound?' she shot at him. 'What would you, a bachelor, know about bringing up children?'

'What my senses tell me,' he said. 'And we drift away from the main point. Married to me, you would have no further financial problems, to name but one advantage.'

Lauren's senses were still reeling. She sat down suddenly in a nearby chair, feeling the shakiness in her legs. A different kind of vertigo, but no less disorientating. She had been here only thirty-six hours. How could she possibly be expected to view this offer of his with equanimity? Marriage with a man she scarcely knew, didn't much like and was even a little afraid of—it didn't bear even thinking about! A purely physical attraction was certainly no basis on which to build a relationship.

'I think you're either quite mad,' she got out, 'or playing some kind of stupid game in order to get me into bed with you. Having a woman turn you down must be a new experience for you.'

'Proposing marriage is a new experience for me,' he came back drily. 'Had I not been drawn to you as a woman, that would be another matter.'

Her head lifted, eyes challenging him. 'You're saying you had marriage in mind even before you kissed me just now?'

The strong mouth slanted. 'I had marriage in mind from the first, but I must confess that desire took precedence a moment ago. I never mastered the art of waiting for what I want.' He paused, gaze holding hers. 'A desire still present.'

'And one which will have to remain unfulfilled,' she retorted. 'I'm neither sleeping with you nor marrying you, Rafael. The whole idea is preposterous!'

His eyes flashed again with that same dangerous light. 'Then I must persuade you.'

Lauren shrank back into the chair as he came purposefully towards her. Bending, he scooped her up in his arms and carried her for a few steps further to a long, high couch, laying her down among the scattered cushions and pinioning her there by the shoulders as he lowered his head to find her mouth with his.

She struggled desperately against the marauding lips, but he simply transferred one hand from shoulder to chin and held her head still. She felt her senses start to swim, the swift spread of heat throughout her body, a curling, muscle-spasming response she was totally unable to control.

Without her volition, her lips softened, began to answer, moving beneath his in mindless exploration. His masculine scent was in her nostrils, filling her with his essence. She slid both her hands over the broad shoulders to draw him closer, breasts swelling to the hard yet erotic pressure of his chest. Her fingers moved up to entangle themselves in the thickness of his hair, convulsing in ecstasy as his tongue entwined with hers.

Francisco had never come close to arousing her to this pitch; she had never known such power of wanting. There was no thought of drawing back now; no thought at all, just pure, uncontrollable need.

Her dress had a long back zip fastener. Rafael lifted her slightly to reach it, drawing it down in one smooth movement and sliding the garment forward until both arms were free of the sleeves. The brassière beneath was a mere wisp of lace which scarcely concealed the full firm swell of her breasts. In a moment, that too was gone, and his hand was exploring the quivering flesh with a touch that drew a smothered gasp to her lips. Her nipples were taut peaks, almost painful in their tingling reaction to his caresses. When he lowered his head to take first one and then the other between his lips, she could scarcely contain her fever.

His sudden withdrawal drew an involuntary protest to her lips, but he had paused only to take off his tuxedo. He followed it with his shirt, ripping open the buttons with scant regard for the tearing silk, and dropping the garment to the floor. His chest was deep and strong, the wiry black curls of hair confined to the centre and tapering down to the waistband of his trousers. The soft lamplight played over oiled muscle, lending a silken sheen to the olive skin. Lauren reached up to savour the emotive masculine flavour of him with delicately flickering tongue.

Rafael said something harsh beneath his breath and put her from him, studying her in intimate detail with a look in his eyes that trapped the breath in her throat. Even then, there was no thought in her mind to stopping any further progression. She wanted him too badly to consider turning back. At the same time, she wanted it to last—the way it had so rarely lasted with Francisco even in the beginning. His lovemaking had been so utterly self-centred, his own satisfaction his only priority.

Rafael was so different. Her enjoyment mattered to him too; that was obvious from the very way in which he was handling her. He was murmuring in Spanish, words she didn't understand and yet somehow knew. The sound of his voice, roughened by passion, was a stimulus in itself.

When he slid her from the couch to lay her on the softness of a rug, she went without protest. When he removed the rest of her clothing to leave her defenceless under his gaze, she knew no reticence. Hands supple, he traced her shape from breast to thigh, lingering there to caress the soft inner skin with a touch so delicate that it made her tremble in anticipation. Her whole body tensed to that first intimate intrusion, though not in rejection. Eyes closed, lips parted, breath coming hard and heavy, she gave her instincts free rein, climaxing on a scream stifled against the back of her hand.

There was a moment of suspension when she thought he had left her. Opening her eyes, she saw him kneeling above her to ready himself, and knew a bare instant of misgiving before the shuddering hunger took over again. She welcomed his descent with eager arms, thrilling to the potent weight of him, the masterful command. The incursion was measured, controlled to a degree that made her clutch at him in a frenzy of sheer urgent need. Her hips lifted in a rhythm of their own, inducing a penetration that turned her whole body fluid and drove her on to abandon all sense of time and place in passionate response.

Her climax this time was even more devastating, followed immediately by thc incredible hot rush of his own release. Slicked with perspiration, she collapsed beneath him, bearing his weight without feeling it, mind void of thought.

Sense and sensibility returned only slowly. Rafael hadn't moved. His head was heavy on her shoulder, his body still joined to hers. She stirred under him, and felt an instant response.

'Another moment, *mi querida*,' he murmured against her ear. 'My recovery is not quite so swift as your own.'

Lauren came suddenly and devastatingly alive to the realisation of where she was and with whom: lying naked on a rug with a man she hadn't even met two days ago! How could she have descended to such a level in such a short time? How could she have lowered herself this far at all, if it came to that? Sheer, unadulterated lust, that was all it was!

'I want you to let me go,' she said on a low, cracked note. 'Please, Rafael!'

His head lifted then, eyes narrowed as they scrutinised her face. 'Too late,' he said. 'You belong to me now. Mine to do with as I wish, whenever I wish!'

'No!' She struggled frantically, ceasing only when her own muscles told her it was useless against his strength. 'I don't want you!' she declared with a venom as much self-directed.

'But you already have me.' His mouth slanted at the look on her face as he made a deliberated movement verifying the fact. 'Would you deny your pleasure in our lovemaking?'

'Don't denigrate the word love!' she spat at him. 'This is sex, nothing more!'

The dark eyes took on a sudden new spark. 'Whatever you might call it, you find it as irresistible as I do myself. There are depths in you, I fancy, that have yet to be explored. I look forward to doing so.'

The gentle yet inexorable thrusting motion of his loins was reaching her despite herself, hammering her heart against her ribcage and causing muscle and sinew to contract in unison. Mind had little control over matter, she realised despairingly, as her senses began to swim again. She was powerless to stop this happening.

He took her swiftly to the peak once more, smothering her cry with the fierce pressure of his lips. The removal of his weight from her what seemed like only moments later left her feeling suddenly cold and bereft. She forced herself to sit upright, avoiding his eyes as she began gathering her discarded clothing, aware only of shame and debasement.

He turned his back on her while she dressed, a gesture she was bound to appreciate regardless of what had passed between them. It was gone three o'clock, she saw from her watch. In another three hours the twins would be awake. They loved it here; they had already said so. But what did they know of the life they would be expected to lead? Once granted the right, Rafael would take total charge of all their lives. Whatever the cost, she had to fight his claim.

Devoid of most of its buttons, the silk shirt hung open across his chest. His hair was roughened by her fingers and curling a little at the ends, lending his face a somewhat younger, less chiselled look. Lauren tried to ignore the surge of adrenalin through her veins as her eyes met his. Nothing on this earth would get her back into those arms of his again, she vowed.

'Later,' he said, 'after we rest, we will discuss the future. The boys may benefit from private tuition for the first year or so.'

'Supposing I did marry you,' Lauren heard herself saying, 'and we had a child? Where would that leave Nicolás and César?'

'As equals in law,' came the unhesitating response. 'And there is no supposing about it.'

Biting back her instinctive denial, she said instead, 'And what of Gabriel?'

'Gabriel has his own inheritance. He stays here at Callahora by choice, not necessity. When he marries, he will have his own home, of course, although he will still continue to share in business matters, if he wishes.'

Rafael got to his feet, proffering a hand to assist her to rise, and drawing an impatient breath when she attempted to refuse it. 'Don't be foolish,' he admonished. 'Pretending to despise me for what you yourself wanted to happen between us is both futile and childish. Be grateful instead that we have such a fine rapport. Our life together will be far from tedious.'

'There's more to marriage than sex!' she flashed. 'Companionship, for one thing. We have nothing at all in common!'

'More, I think, than you had with my brother,' he returned. Reaching down, he yanked her bodily to her feet, holding her there in front of him to look deep into her eyes. 'You must learn to obey me, *mi querida*. A man must be master in the home.'

'You're out of date,' she rejoined with cutting inflexion. 'Women are equals where I come from!'

His smile was brief and derisive. 'Women will never be the equals of men, no matter how you try. Your physical form alone makes it impossible.'

'Size and strength aren't the only criteria,' she countered. 'I'll obey *no* man.'

'Perhaps,' he said, 'it was my brother's failure to gain your respect that caused the marriage itself to fail so drastically.'

'Meaning he might have left other women alone if I'd shown a little more subservience?' Lauren queried bitterly. 'Like hell!'

The hands still holding her tautened their grasp. 'I'll have no wife of mine using such language!'

'I'm *not* your wife!' she flung at him. 'Nor will I be! You can't force me to marry you—any more than you can force Gabriel to marry Alicia!'

Rafael went suddenly very still, face like granite. 'What would you know of that?'

She was already regretting the hasty words, but it was too late to retract. She sent a mental apology to Gabriel for betraying his confidence before attempting to qualify her statement. 'It's only too obvious that he's reluctant.'

'In order to perceive this reluctance, you must have had premature knowledge of the marriage arrangement itself,' said Rafael. 'When did Gabriel tell you of it?'

'About an hour ago,' she acknowledged resignedly. 'While you were seeing the Floreses off. But I'd guessed earlier what the situation might be. He's entitled to make his own choice of bride. He doesn't love Alicia.'

'It isn't necessary for him to love her, nor she him,' came the intolerant reply. 'The promise was made a long time ago, and must be fulfilled. The honour of the family is at stake.'

'And that, of course, is far more important than your brother's happiness!' Lauren was too incensed to heed the warning glitter in the dark eyes. 'I was right before. You *are* a tyrant! You've no feeling for anyone or anything beyond your own interests!'

'That,' he clipped, 'is enough! One more word from you on the subject, and you will have reason to regret it!' He released her abruptly, face taut. 'Now, go to bed.'

To defy that command would be tempting providence, Lauren decided with reluctance. It was difficult, looking at him now, to believe that he was the same man who had held her so passionately in his arms a short time ago; the man who had given her such pleasure as she had never dreamed of. She knew him intimately, yet she didn't know him at all.

'I said to go to bed,' he repeated in a last-time-of-telling tone of voice, and she went, leaving him standing there.

The castle was silent as the grave. Lauren climbed the stairs quickly, more than half afraid he would come after her. Reaching her room, she closed the door and locked it, standing for a moment with her back against the wood and her gaze fixed unseeingly on the moonlit window.

No rape would be necessary, Rafael had said, and it hadn't been. She had succumbed to him with barely a struggle. She could still feel the pressure of his body, the tingling certainty of his hands on her skin. She felt ravished by him, stripped of every ounce of self-respect. How did she face him again after what had passed between them?

More to the point, how did she get away from this place? She *and* the twins, because she certainly wasn't leaving without them. Gabriel might help. He would have to help. He was the only one she could turn to.

CHAPTER FIVE

SLEEP came eventually, but not, it seemed, for long. Lying there in the darkness, Lauren wondered if the sound that had woken her had been reality or just part of her dream.

The latter had faded now; she could recall no detail of it apart from a sense of disquiet. Sitting up, she reached for the travel alarm on the bedside table, seeing from its illuminated face that it was barely five-thirty. Memory returned in a heart-jerking rush. Not three hours ago she had been with Rafael, had given herself to Rafael. The ache in her body was tangible proof of *that* reality.

Her brother-in-law. That made it even worse. There was no excuse for her weakness. It was doubtful if he would actually have used force if she had said no. She had allowed herself to be used by a man driven only by sexual desire—a man devoid of the finer emotions. Like Francisco himself, Rafael Javierre de Quiros put his own interests first and foremost. Only he needn't imagine that offering her marriage was going to alter anything. She had no intention of putting her head in yet another noose.

The disquiet still lingering was somehow disconnected from her present thoughts. She hadn't looked in on the twins on coming to bed for fear of wakening them, but something prompted her now to take the risk. Switching on a lamp, she slid from the bed and reached for her wrap. It would only take a moment. If she woke them it was unlikely that they'd go to sleep again, but then she doubted if she would sleep again herself. Occupying their minds for the next hour or so would also occupy her own.

She had forgotten about locking her door. Turning the key in the lock caused a slight grating sound. Feet clad in soft slippers, she made no sound at all in crossing the few feet of stone floor to the other room.

At first sight, the two empty beds made little impression. Only on realising that the boys weren't in the room at all did fear begin to rear its head. Outside again, she hesitated at the spiral stairs, uncertain whether to go up or down. Her instincts told her to mount rather than to descend, because that was new territory for the twins, and therefore far more interesting than below.

She went up as quickly as she could, pausing only momentarily at Rafael's landing. If they had come up here at all, the narrower spiral of steps leading to the turret roof would have proved the greater draw. Heart hammering into her throat, she continued on up, holding on to the rough stone wall for support and hoping against hope that she was wrong. There was so much danger up here, so little protection from the dizzying heights beyond the parapet.

There was no moon now, but the starlight itself was bright enough to see by when she emerged at last into the open air. Every nerve in her body froze as her eyes took in the very scene she had dreaded. César had climbed into one of the embrasures and was standing there laughing down at his brother in triumph, a small, pyjama-clad figure utterly devoid of fear.

'I'm the king of the castle!' he crowed.

If she shouted, Lauren thought desperately, she might startle him into taking a fatal step backwards. She had to stay calm and collected and pretend that nothing untoward was happening.

'So here you are,' she said. 'I thought you might be.' Her voice was wavering; she made a supreme effort to control it. 'Time to go back to bed now.'

'We aren't tired any more,' said Nicolás. 'And it's my turn to be king now.' He reached up a hand to tug at his brother's pyjama leg. 'Come on down, Zar.'

'In a minute.' César was obviously reluctant to relinquish his vantage point. 'Come and look, Mummy,' he called, turning about to peer into the depths. 'You can't see the ground at all!'

Without even thinking about it, Lauren propelled herself across the intervening space to grab the small body about the waist, yanking him to her with such force that she lost her own balance and stumbled backwards on to hard, unyielding stone. She scarcely felt the pain, conscious only of the overwhelming relief in having her son safe in her arms.

'My turn now,' cried Nicolás, entering into the spirit of a good game and preparing to climb where his brother had been. 'Get ready to catch me!'

'Stop right there!' Sharp and assertive, the command froze him in his tracks. Still sitting where she had landed, with César held tight despite his struggles to be free, Lauren turned her head to see Rafael emerge from the doorway. He was wearing a short silk robe, his legs bare beneath it. There was light enough now to see the grimness of his expression.

'Come away from the parapet,' he ordered. 'Nicolás, isn't it?'

Looking suddenly uncertain, Nicolás obeyed. Rafael bent to lift César from Lauren's arms and deposit him on his feet before hoisting her upright. 'Are you hurt?' he demanded.

She shook her head, too unnerved to speak. The only too familiar trembling overtook her at the realisation of where she was. The door seemed a hundred yards away, the very stone beneath her feet unstable.

Ushering both boys ahead of him, Rafael took her around the waist and guided her to safety. Lauren resisted the urge to clutch at him when he released her to view the two diminutive figures, who awaited developments with more interest than trepidation.

'You will walk down the stairs behind your mother,' he said. 'And with caution.'

Lauren made a small sound of protest swiftly stilled by the look he turned on her. As she had the previous time, she began the descent with a hand on his shoulder to steady her, making sure that the twins were following behind. The two of them were as sure-footed as mountain goats. Giggling, they counted every step to a slow cadence that brought a reluctant smile to Lauren's own lips. They knew their numbers, the way they knew so many things. She couldn't help but feel a degree of pride in their accomplishments—even in their boldness.

Rafael made no attempt to halt at his floor but carried straight on down to theirs. Neither child had been wearing slippers, and their feet had to be filthy, but he didn't hesitate, ordering them into bed in a tone that sent the two of them scurrying to obey.

'You stay there,' he said, 'until you're given permission to get up. And never again are you to venture alone on to the roof. Is that understood?'

'Why?' asked Nicolás, recovering his tongue.

'Because it's dangerous,' Rafael answered.

'Why?' asked César, not about to be left out.

'Because you could fall and be killed,' came the flat response. 'Go to sleep now.'

Both boys slid obediently beneath the sheets, although Lauren doubted if it was to sleep. She went almost defiantly to kiss each small face before following Rafael from the room.

'Why did you not call me?' he demanded as soon as the door was closed. 'Why go up there alone knowing how it would be for you?'

'There wasn't time,' she denied. 'I had this feeling they were in danger.'

'A danger that need not have arisen had they been warned of it in advance.'

'I don't want them developing my fear of heights,' Lauren responded. 'In any case, warning them would only have aroused their curiosity the more. They've no real concept of danger.'

'Then it's high time that they acquired one.'

'I already told you...' she began.

'I know what you told me,' he said. 'Your acrophobia is personal, and unlikely to be passed on. You could overcome it to a great extent by gradual desensitisation.'

Reaction to the fright she had received, mingled with resentment of his attitude, put a snap in her voice. 'Since when did you qualify as a therapist?'

'It takes no special qualification to speak common sense,' Rafael returned shortly. 'For the moment, however, the concern must be centred on Nicolás and César. They must learn to follow a few simple but effective rules. First and foremost, there will be no more wandering around in the middle of the night. If they awaken, they stay in their room and read, or play with their toys.'

'They've already read all the books I brought with us,' she said, 'and they don't have any toys here.'

'So today we all of us drive down to Marbella to choose some. That is,' he added, 'if we have the energy left to do so after so much activity tonight.'

Meeting his eyes, Lauren felt the colour flood her cheeks. It wasn't just the events of the past few minutes to which he was referring.

'You blush so beautifully,' he said on a note of amusement, putting paid to her hope that he wouldn't have noticed in the light coming through the single narrow window. 'A very virginal reaction in a woman married five years.'

'Married to your brother,' she reminded him with a coolness she was far from feeling. 'And him dead only a few months. If *you* have no shame, it doesn't mean I can't feel any.'

'By your own admission, you had no feeling left for him,' came the unmoved response, 'so there can be little depth of sorrow. I mourn the man he might have been, not the one he became. The living must continue with their lives.'

'But not necessarily together.' Lauren steeled herself to say it. 'I won't marry you, Rafael. What happened last night was a mistake I've no intention of repeating.'

There was a brief moment when she feared he was about to seize her. Her bedroom was only a step away, and the children in too close proximity for any resistance on her part. She drew in a shallow breath that was only partly of relief when he shrugged and gave a faint smile.

'We shall see. You have more than an hour before sunrise. I'd advise that you use it to rest. On Saturdays I take breakfast later myself, so I'll see you then. We'll leave for Marbella at nine, and spend the whole day at the coast. Nicolás and César will enjoy the beach.'

He was moving away before she could answer—if there was an answer. He had it all mapped out, she thought helplessly as he vanished up the stairs. Even if she tried making a break for it if the opportunity arose, what then? She had little money, no return tickets, and who was going to help her?

If even remotely upset by their uncle's stern admonishment, the twins showed little sign of it when Lauren went in to them at seven. They were playing a game of 'I spy' in their usual amicable fashion.

'Uncle Rafael is taking us all to the coast today,' she said brightly. 'You'll be able to play on the sands and paddle in the sea.'

'Like at Southend?' asked Nicolás.

'Better than that,' she promised, and felt bound to add, 'You don't really deserve it after last night. You must do as Uncle Rafael says, and stay here in your room while it's dark.'

'We like Uncle Rafael,' announced César, surprisingly. 'We want him to be our daddy.'

Lauren gazed at the pair of them in total disarray. 'You hardly know him,' was all she could find to say.

'He looks like Daddy,' said Nicolás, as if that clinched the matter.

'There's more to it than that.' Lauren tried desperately to find the words they might understand. 'In order for Uncle Rafael to be your daddy, I would have to be married to him.'

The two of them regarded her unblinkingly. 'What's married?' asked César.

'Well, like Daddy and I were,' she began haltingly. 'When two people...love each other, they want to be together always, so they sign a piece of paper that makes them husband and wife.'

'Don't you love Uncle Rafael?' asked Nicolás.

Her heart jerked painfully. What she felt towards the man in question came closer to hatred than love, but she could scarcely tell them that. 'Not enough to marry him,' she prevaricated. 'It takes an awful lot of love for that.'

'Did you love Daddy that much?'

The voice was César's, the question innocent, the pain it engendered a stab wound. 'Of course,' she lied, unable to do anything else in the circumstances. She briskened her voice. 'And it's time you were dressed. We don't want Uncle Rafael to go without us, do we?'

The mere possibility was enough to drive all other thoughts from their minds for the moment, but Lauren doubted if it would be forgotten completely. Why they should have taken such a shine to a man who had so far done little but lay down the law she couldn't imagine. Forbidding as he must have appeared to them such a short time ago, it seemed to have left no bad impression.

Both brothers were already at table when they got down. Lauren's apology for their tardiness was waved aside by Rafael without concern.

'We have no timetable to keep,' he declared.

Fresh coffee was brought to his order, and the twins settled with their cereal. To Lauren's relief, they made no attempt to reopen the discussion abandoned upstairs, but chatted excitedly about the forthcoming trip.

'I would very much like to take you to Burgo this evening,' said Gabriel when his brother went to fetch a jacket before leaving. 'There's a fine discothèque, with excellent music.'

'I think I'll probably be far too tired after a day out for that kind of thing,' Lauren answered gently, 'but thanks for the thought.'

'You think I should take Alicia if I take anyone at all?' he asked on a wry note.

She hesitated before replying, aware of treading on tricky ground. 'It isn't my place to tell you what you should or shouldn't do,' she said at length. 'You're the only one able to make that decision. All I would say is to make it sooner rather than later. Alicia deserves to know where she stands.'

Rafael's return cut short any response Gabriel might have been about to make. Wearing deep blue trousers and open-necked shirt, with a beautifully tailored jacket in paler blue, the former set Lauren's pulses leaping. She had chosen to wear white today in a simple little cotton-mixture suit she hoped would prove equal to whatever the day turned up. Her hair was fastened back into the nape of her neck with a large tortoiseshell slide, her face free of make-up outside of a smear of eye-shadow and a pale pink lipstick.

Today they were to travel in the roomy and luxurious saloon in which Gabriel had collected them from the airport. Less than two days ago, Lauren realised with a sense of shock as she slid into the front passenger-seat. So much had happened since then. More than she cared to think about right now.

Except that it was difficult to do anything else with Rafael seated at her side. Roomy as the car was, he was still too close. She could see the line of his thigh from the corner of her eye, the stretch of blue linen over firm muscle as he depressed the clutch to change gear. She had felt the strength of those same muscles in intimate detail last night; her stomach fluttered at the memory.

She wanted him again right now; there was no getting away from it. Only that was no basis for marriage.

Confined by childproof locks, the twins contented themselves with a noses-pressed-on-glass appraisal of the scenery they had missed on the previous journey. Lauren kept her own gaze averted from the road edge, trying not to think about the terrifying drops. When the whole spread of coastline finally came into view, she was diverted enough to forget her fears in admiration of the sunlit panorama.

Backed by pine-clad hills, the one-time fishing village of Marbella had expanded into a sizeable township. Although modern and ugly in the outer reaches, the old town still survived at the centre in narrow white traffic-free lanes. The Plaza de las Naranjas was planted with orange trees and set out with tables belonging to the various restaurants. At night in high season, Rafael said, the whole square would be thronged with diners, the demarcation lines between establishments marked only by differences in the colours of table-coverings and umbrellas. A meeting place for all, wherever they came from.

The toyshop to which he took them was in the modern section. Nicolás and César could hardly believe it when he invited them to choose whatever they wanted from the huge selection presented. For several minutes they were both of them too awestruck to do anything but look.

'It's too much,' Lauren protested, watching them pick up first one thing and then another. 'They don't even know where to start!'

'Then perhaps we should help them to choose,' Rafael suggested, ignoring the implied criticism. 'A train set, perhaps, to begin with. And a football each.'

'They can only play with one at a time,' she pointed out.

'Not necessarily.' He moved to join the two boys, indicating the superb model-railway already set out on a table near by. 'Would you like one of these in your bedroom?'

The invitation was all it took. Lauren tried her best to conceal her emotions as the three of them proceeded to carve up the whole shop between them. It was no use telling herself that Rafael was simply currying favour with her sons, because they had already expressed their feelings towards him. Having him take any kind of interest in them at all was novelty enough compared with their father's lack of it, she supposed. Francisco would never have dreamed of taking them to a toyshop—or any place else, for that matter—and discipline had always been her province.

Rafael was probably right in thinking that she hadn't made a very good job of it, she acknowledged ruefully. There had to be a happy medium between too much and too little repression.

She joined in eventually, unable to stand by and watch any longer. The twins welcomed her with beaming delight, while Rafael afforded her an approving smile of his own. Other adult shoppers looked on indulgently, other children enviously, as the list grew. Some of the things they were to take with them in the car, the rest would be delivered. Choosing which to take and which to leave proved the most difficult task of all.

It was gone one o'clock already, Lauren was amazed to learn when they emerged at last into the open air. They would eat lunch before visiting the beach, Rafael declared. The buckets and spades just acquired would not disappear in the meantime.

Nicolás and César accepted the proposal without undue reluctance. They had already learned that what their uncle said was to be taken as meant. Lauren got back into the car feeling that her position was fast becoming subverted. On her own, she would have taken the line of least resistance and made do with a hot dog, she knew, and knowing it didn't help.

They left the town to head into the foothills for a few minutes, turning eventually through double wrought-iron gates to draw up before a small but imposing-looking building fronted by flower gardens.

A hotel, Lauren realised on entering the elegant vestibule. A costly one too, if she were any judge. Only on hearing the respectful greeting afforded Rafael by the receptionist did it dawn on her that this was one of the Quiros hotels themselves.

The restaurant was full to overflowing, but a table was procured for the four of them out on the terrace with its magnificent view of the coastline. Nicolás and César were entranced, Lauren herself scarcely less so. She felt like royalty.

Obviously known by sight if not acquaintance by many of the clientele, Rafael drew speculative glances from all sides. With the boys looking so much like their uncle, it was inevitable that certain conclusions would be drawn, Lauren wryly supposed. Conclusions that would in no way be eradicated by their marriage, unless he went out of his way to publicise their true relationship, which seemed unlikely. In Rafael's eyes, it would be no one's concern but his own.

But she wasn't going to marry him, was she? He couldn't, she told herself firmly, bribe *her* into compliance!

He could, however, lull her into a state of relaxation, she found over the following hour. Not just an outstandingly handsome companion but a captivating one too. He talked about books, about music, about everything under the sun except the situation she still couldn't bring herself to contemplate with any equanimity. He had made love to her, but he didn't love her. She had had enough of that kind of relationship with his brother.

It took a woman in the party that came to sit at a nearby table to remind her of Nina Ortega. There was the same cold beauty, the same air of arrogance. Noting her sudden change of expression, Rafael followed her glance, his mouth acquiring a slant.

'Alike but not the same,' he said. 'Nina has never been to La Trucha.'

The twins appeared to have their attention wholly on their ice-cream sundaes. Lauren said quietly, 'What exactly is she to you?'

'Of little consequence,' he replied.

'Then why was she invited last night?'

He shrugged. 'A gesture, no more.'

'But you didn't care to see her with another man,' Lauren observed, and saw his jawline tauten.

'I care to see no woman in the company of Xaviour Ríos. Your own senses must surely have warned you he is a man not to be trusted.'

'I found him quite charming,' she lied with deliberation.

'Then your perception is shallower than I believed.'

Drawn by the sudden change in atmosphere, the twins were taking an interest in the conversation. Lauren bit back her sharp retort and found a bland smile. 'I'm sure you know best.'

'We finished our ice-cream,' said César, seizing on the pause. 'Is it time to go to the beach now?'

Rafael laughed, humour apparently restored. 'Just as soon as we finish our coffee.'

Another time, such a delay would have invoked protests, Lauren knew, but, although obviously fidgeting to be up and away, the two made no verbal objections. Rafael could control them so easily; he didn't even need to raise his voice. An instinctive recognition of authority, she supposed. Not that she liked having the reins taken from her hands, even if she had been holding them a little too loosely. They were *her* sons. She wouldn't allow him to take them from her!

With coffee finally drunk, they got their way. Rafael drove back through the town to park as close as possible to the beach. The sky was clear, the sun hot. He left his jacket in the car, and rolled his shirt sleeves, earning himself yet another obvious accolade from the twins who preferred casual to dress-up themselves any day of the week.

Lauren was wearing a straw-coloured cotton bustier under her own jacket for coolness. She felt self-conscious with her shoulders bared, but Rafael seemed to approve. She had brought a pair of mules along to exchange for the dressier high-heeled sandals which were hardly suitable for walking in sand.

Instead of one long and boring stretch, the beach was shaped to form a series of small lagoons. There were plenty of other people lying, sitting or walking on the sand. Rafael chose a spot close enough to the water for the twins to paddle under supervision, and spread the rug he had brought from the car.

'You seem to have thought of everything,' said Lauren, trying to keep any hint of sarcasm from her voice. 'One would think you were used to occasions like this.'

'One would be wrong,' he mocked mildly. 'The requirements are simple enough. Next time we bring the children to the beach we'll also bring a picnic.'

'It's rather a long way to come just for that, isn't it?' she suggested.

His shrug made light of the matter. 'Not as far, I believe, as you would travel in England from where you lived.'

'Live!' The correction was sharp. 'It isn't past tense yet—and never will be, if I have anything to do with it!'

Shoes and socks hastily discarded, the twins were already in the water. Rafael kept his eyes on them as he said softly, 'Why do you continue to fight me? Would you try to deny what you feel?'

Lauren drew in a shaky breath. 'If you're talking about last night, it meant nothing. I—I lost my head, that's all. And I'd prefer to forget it.'

His laugh came low. 'An occasion *I* find impossible to forget. And one,' he added, 'I intend to repeat. Tonight I think we must spend together—the whole of it. I wish to sleep with you in my arms, *amada*, to waken with you by my side and make love to you in the dawn light. I want to know you the way no man before has ever known you to have you know me as intimately as it is possible for a woman to know a man.'

Her heart was hammering against her ribs like a wild bird against bars, the blood singing in her ears. Her voice when she found it sounded totally unlike her own. 'I already do.'

'No,' he denied. 'You only know my body. And not even that the way you will. Tonight——'

'Stop it!' Her breath was ragged. 'It isn't going to happen again. I won't let it happen again!'

'Even though you want it to happen as much as I do myself?' He shook his head, smile mocking her denials. 'You will have to convince me beyond any shadow of doubt that you find my caresses unwelcome before I begin to reconsider our future relationship.'

'There isn't going to be any future relationship,' she said desperately. 'Not the kind you mean, at any rate. You can't force me into this marriage.'

'I can persuade you,' he responded. 'If only in your sons' interests. They respond to me already as a father figure.'

It was true, but she couldn't bring herself to like it. Francisco had left their upbringing almost entirely to her; Rafael would expect total control. And not only where the twins were concerned either. If she did consent to marry him, her life would no longer be her own.

On the other hand, came the sneaking thought, there would be compensations. Where else was she going to find a man who could make her feel the way Rafael made her feel? Where else, if it came to that, was she going to find any man willing to take on two children? It was all very well to tell herself that she didn't need a man in *her* life, but was that fair on the boys? Looking at them now, splashing away happily in the shallows, considering the differences in the life they were living here and that they would be living back home, the answer had to be no.

As if sensing some change in her, Rafael had the wisdom to let the whole subject drop for the moment. Seizing a spade, he began to dig a hole. Seeing him, the twins came running eagerly back to join in.

'Can we build a castle just like yours?' asked Nicolás.

'Like ours,' Rafael corrected casually. 'It's your home too now.'

Two pairs of eyes shone like stars. 'We're going to live there always?'

'Always,' came the firm declaration. His glance sought Lauren's, challenging her to disagree. 'Ask your *mamá*.'

He had her in a cleft stick, Lauren acknowledged with mingled emotions. To defy him now would cause untold confusion. 'It seems so,' she said, trying to put a good face on it.

'And are you and Uncle Rafael going to be married so that he can be our daddy?' insisted César.

It was Rafael himself who answered before Lauren could even form the words. 'Yes, we are.'

'That's all right, then,' said Nicolás, and turned back to more immediately vital matters. 'I'm going to build our tower first.'

Watching the three of them set to, dark heads so close as they worked, Lauren was aware of mingled emotions. Rafael would be a good father. He had the twins' interests at heart. As a husband, that was another matter. The physical side of marriage was only a part. How would she cope with the rest?

CHAPTER SIX

IT WAS almost six o'clock when they reached Callahora. Gabriel greeted them with ill-concealed disgruntlement. Undeterred, the twins gave him a breathless account of their day before disappearing up to their bedroom to start sorting out the toys and books they had brought back with them. The train set was to be delivered on Monday, along with the rest.

After this, what on earth would they do at Christmas? Lauren wondered, leaving the two of them to enjoy themselves until bedtime. More to the point, how would things be by Christmas? She still felt dazed by the speed with which matters had progressed. There was so much to think about. Their home in England, for one thing. She would have to return in order to arrange the sale.

The very idea gave rise to fresh qualms. In effect, she would be severing all links with her homeland. It was unlikely too that Rafael would allow her to take the boys back with her, even if she swore to return. Given half an opportunity, she probably wouldn't return either, although she was bound to admit that the thought of never seeing him again wasn't exactly pleasurable.

If the truth were known, she reflected wryly, she was being carried along as much by her own needs as those of the twins. In Rafael's arms she was a different person—passsionate, responsive, free of all restraints. He made her feel a complete woman.

Perhaps Francisco would have made more of an effort with their marriage had she been able to respond to him the same way. Even in the beginning she had held a part of herself back. Yet it would only have been a pretence at the best, and an unenlightened one at that. How could she have acted what she had never experienced?

The knock on her bedroom door brought her heart leaping into her throat. Tonight we spend together, Rafael had said, but that wasn't to say he wouldn't anticipate an earlier assignation too. 'Mine to do with as I wish, whenever I wish'; those had been his very words. Refute that claim though she might, she couldn't deny a certain thrill.

She could neither deny a certain disappointment when she opened the door to find Gabriel standing there.

'I came,' he said, 'to ask you again if you will accompany me to Burgo?'

Lauren hesitated before replying, not at all sure how she *should* answer. It was up to Rafael to put his brother in the picture. Truth to tell, she couldn't face doing it herself.

'Discos really aren't my taste,' she prevaricated. 'They never were, I'm afraid.'

'Then we go somewhere else,' he offered eagerly. 'To Ronda, perhaps?'

'I don't think so.' She paused again, reluctant to hurt his feelings with a flat refusal, then added tentatively, 'You should talk with Rafael.'

Dark brows drew together in a sudden scowl. 'Has he forbidden you to be with me?'

'No, he hasn't!' Her sharpness was a rejection of the idea itself. 'Just talk to him!'

He was still standing there when she closed the door, his face reflecting a dawning enlightenment. Waiting, Lauren heard his footsteps moving towards the staircase, and drew a sigh of mingled relief and regret. She had handled that badly. There had been no need for the acrimony. If Gabriel simply suspected his brother of putting in a prior claim on her time, which was likely, then he was in for a shock.

The shock wouldn't be confined to him either, she realised. Once released, the news would spread like wildfire. Except that the marriage was hardly going to be imminent, so it was unnecessary for anyone else to be told as yet. In fact, Rafael might well have intended to keep his brother in the dark too, until he decided the time was ripe for an announcement.

In which case, he should have said, Lauren defended herself. She had enough to contend with without trying to keep Gabriel at arm's length.

The *salón* was empty when she went down. The memory of what had happened here last night sent a wave of heat through her. Initially she had hated Rafael—or she had told herself she did. Now, she wasn't sure what it was she felt, outside of the obvious. Not hate any longer, but certainly not love. She was betwixt and between, and likely to stay there.

The subject of her thoughts arrived bare moments later. Wearing black silk shirt and white trousers, he looked more casual but just as devastating as he had the previous night. He eyed her choice of amber skirt and matching long-sleeved blouse with clear approval.

'You look delectable,' he said. 'But then, you always do. What would you like to drink?'

'Sherry, please,' she said, plumping for the first thing that came to mind. She watched him pour the golden liquid, surprised when he filled two glasses. 'I didn't imagine sherry to be to your taste,' she commented when he brought them across to where she sat.

'You consider it purely a woman's drink?' he asked with a quirk of an eyebrow, and smiled to see her hesitation. 'In Spain we draw no such demarcation lines. Jerez, the home of all fine sherries, is only a few miles away. I must take you to visit the *bodega* of a friend. Felipe has an English wife too, along with a son close to the twins' own age, and a daughter two years younger.'

'No doubt they knew one another a whole lot longer than two days,' Lauren was moved to murmur.

'Their circumstances were different from ours, certainly,' he returned. There was a pause, and a change of tone when he spoke again. 'You lost little time in telling Gabriel of our intentions.'

'I told him nothing,' she denied. 'Except to talk to you, that is. He wanted me to go to Burgo with him. What other excuse could I make?'

'A simple no should have been enough.'

'Not without hurting his feelings.'

'His feelings are not your concern.' The tone was harder now. 'He had no business asking you to go with him at all.'

'Because of Alicia?' Lauren refused to allow the spark in his eyes to deflect her. 'You already know my views on that score.'

'Which alters nothing. If Gabriel fails to fulfil the contract, he will no longer have a home at Callahora.'

She gazed at him in disbelief. 'You can't be serious!'

'Certainly I'm serious.' He sounded it too. 'And there will be no interference from you either. Our ways are not your ways.'

'They're not even twentieth century!' she burst out. 'Why should Gabriel be landed with a wife he doesn't want simply because someone decided for him when he was too young to have a say in the matter?'

Still standing, glass in hand, Rafael regarded her with intolerance. 'I refuse to argue with you,' he declared flatly. 'The subject is closed.'

'And I refuse to be quiet just because you say so!' she snapped back. 'If it's a doormat you're after, you're looking in the wrong place!'

Anger gave way unexpectedly to a somewhat grim amusement. 'You have the Latin temperament if not the blood,' he observed. 'I always believed Englishwomen were lacking in passion of any kind. Take care, however, not to press me too far.'

Or else what? she was tempted to demand, but the look in his eyes prompted discretion rather than valour. With his masculine pride at stake, there was no telling what he might do if she continued to provoke him.

'You begin to acquire wisdom at last,' he commented drily when she remained silent. 'A good sign for our future together.'

'I haven't said I'll marry you yet,' Lauren felt moved to remind him. 'Not in so many words.'

'But you failed to correct me when I told Nicolás and César we were to be married,' he countered. 'Would you refuse them also?'

'They're too young to know what it's all about.'

'Not too young to know that something is missing from their lives.' The pause was weighted, the lean features inflexible. 'I can't force you into marriage. Neither, as I said before, can I keep you here against your will, but I can and will claim my brother's sons. The choice is entirely your own.'

Gazing at him, Lauren hardly knew what she felt. Marriage with a man so dominant would be no bed of roses for sure, yet at the same time she was forced to acknowledge that his very assertiveness was an integral part of his attraction. Learning how to handle him would be a challenge of the kind no yes-man could provide.

And what was the alternative? She could fight his claim on the twins, but a Spanish court would almost certainly consider their prospects here far more advantageous than any she could offer them back home. Which they were, of course. They'd also accepted that Rafael was going to be their new daddy. Could she find the heart to tell them now that it wasn't going to be?

'Perhaps this may help you make up your mind,' said Rafael on a softer note. He took the glass from her unresisting hand to deposit it along with his own on a nearby table, and drew her to her feet, moulding her body against him in a way that sent the blood racing through her veins. His mouth found hers, nuzzling her lips apart, his tongue seeking, tasting, drawing instant response. Arms sliding of their own volition about his neck, Lauren clung to him, conscious only of the heat spreading through her, of the fervent desire to be closer—to feel the warmth and texture of his skin, the rippling power of muscle, the tingling brush of his body hair against her breasts. In this way, she was wholly his. She knew it, and he knew it too.

It took her a moment or two to pull herself together when he finally let her go. He was breathing a little heavier himself, but still in control.

'We must wait a while for satisfaction,' he said with regret. 'This is not the time to indulge. Tonight I come to your bed.'

'You're taking it for granted that the door won't be locked,' she whispered, and saw a smile touch his lips.

'If the door is locked, it will be unlocked. You can no more resist what lies between us than I can myself. To-night, *amada*, we fly to the stars!'

Coming from an Englishman, such a statement would have sounded ridiculous, Lauren thought, but from Rafael it was sheer poetry—exciting poetry! The deeper, more lasting emotions seemed immaterial right now.

'So tell me,' he prompted. 'Let me hear you say the words.'

Once she had, there would be no going back on them, she knew; she would be committed. All the same, she found herself doing it. 'All right, I'll marry you.'

Something in him seemed to relax. The hand reaching out to caress her cheek was almost tender. 'Such a struggle!'

Such a waste of time and effort, was what he really meant, Lauren guessed. He had known full well what her answer would be. She refused to think about the consequences. From now on she was going to live each moment as it came.

She made no comment when Gabriel failed to put in an appearance at dinner. Sympathetic though she felt towards him, he had to sort out his own life. Tonight her seat was at Rafacl's side rather than at the far end of the table.

'Formality belongs to formal occasions,' he said when she mentioned it. 'Conversation would be difficult with the length of the table between us.'

'I've no objection,' she disclaimed hastily. 'I prefer it this way myself.'

His smile was slow. 'You like to be close to me?'

Her pulses quickened as his hand stroked lightly along her thigh. She caught it and held it, registering the amusement in his eyes with a reluctant little smile of her own. 'Don't do that—please!'

'Why?' he asked. 'Do you not enjoy my touch?'

'There's a time and place,' she said. 'Right now is for eating.'

'The body requires more than one kind of sustenance,' came the taunting reply. 'I must teach you to relax your inhibitions a little more.' He laughed indulgently as the colour rose in her cheeks. 'So much spirit, yet so easily embarrassed!'

'I can't help it,' she acknowledged. 'I'm just not used to...'

'To a desire that takes little heed of the clock?' he suggested as her voice trailed away. 'My brother was surely no laggard in his appetites?'

The flush deepened. 'There was nothing of that nature between us for two years before his death,' she admitted. 'I wouldn't have wanted there to be.'

'Because of the other women?' The tone was neutral.

'Partly.' She hesitated before tagging on thickly, 'He considered me frigid.'

'And were you?'

Lauren gave him a swift sideways glance. 'Do I seem so to you?'

'Far from it,' he returned with reassuring certainty. 'But I'm not my brother. If he failed to make you respond to him, that was his inadequacy, not yours.'

She swallowed on the sudden lump in her throat. 'You're a great comfort.'

'Also a very good lover,' he appended with a humorous twitch of his lips. 'You would agree?'

Instinct lowered her eyes in mock submissiveness. 'Unsurpassed!'

His laugh held a genuine appreciation. 'You learn fast, *mi querida*!'

Mi querida. My darling, in English; even she knew that. A sentiment which tripped too glibly from his lips to be anything but practised, yet it still held impact. One day, Lauren promised herself in sudden determination, he would say it to her alone, and mean it. She would oust all other women from his mind!

An ambitious project considering her lack of expertise in holding a man's interest, came the following, somewhat dispiriting thought, but worth a try. What did she have to lose?

Rafael made no further mention of his intentions when they parted at midnight. He would wait, Lauren guessed, until the household was quiet before coming to her. At least, that was what she hoped. She wanted his love-making so badly that it hurt to leave him at all. Her whole body was on fire with the need to be in his arms again.

She looked in on the twins before going to her own room. Nicolás was fast asleep, one arm wrapped tightly about a new teddy bear. Lauren straightened the rumpled sheets and bent to kiss the smooth forehead beneath its shock of black hair, before turning to César's bed.

At first glance, he too appeared to be sleeping the sleep of total peace and contentment. Only on touching his forehead did she realise he was burning hot. He moaned when she moved him, but didn't open his eyes. Panic stirred in her, dampened down by sheer force of will. Children ran fevers at the drop of a hat; they'd both done it at times.

Yes, but not like this, came the response. This was something far more serious than a simple temperature fluctuation.

Leaving him as she had found him, she ran from the room and made for the stairs. Rafael was still fully dressed when she burst into his bedroom without bothering to knock. He looked at her with lifted brows.

'I was to come to you,' he said. 'However——'

'It's César. He's ill!' she said urgently. 'Really ill!'

Expression abruptly altered, he lost no time on questions. He led the way downstairs again, took one look at César, and came to an instant decision.

'We have a doctor among our guests at present,' he said. 'It will be far quicker to ask him to attend than to send for one of our own. Wait here while I fetch him.'

She wasn't going anywhere else for sure, Lauren thought. Sitting down on the edge of the bed, she resisted the urge to gather her son in her arms, contenting herself instead with stroking the burning forehead. He was restless now; she wasn't sure whether that was a good sign or not. Just don't let it be anything serious, she prayed. Both children had drunk only bottled water while they'd been here, so it was hardly likely to be a tummy bug. In any case, the symptoms weren't right.

It seemed an age before Rafael returned. He had an older man wearing a dressing-gown in tow. The latter took Lauren's place on the bed to conduct his examination. He made a thorough job of it, whoever he was, she had to acknowledge. She waited with fast-beating heart for the verdict.

'The child appears to have been bitten by something,' he announced, indicating an angry red patch on one small arm. 'The fever is his body's way of fighting the infection. His temperature is below the danger level, so providing it isn't allowed to rise any further he should be fine. I'd recommend sponging him down with warm water and allowing his skin to dry naturally. The evaporation will cool him down. With walls this thick,' he added, 'the air temperature in here is kept pretty constant, which is all to the good.'

'You're sure he's going to be all right?' Lauren insisted as he rose from his seat.

The smile itself was reassuring. 'Children are surprisingly resilient. I'd lay a bet that he'll be up and about again in the morning as right as rain.'

Almost as if hearing the prediction, César opened his eyes, focusing in confusion on the group at the side of his bed. 'Mummy,' he whimpered, 'I don't feel very well.'

Lauren sat down again and took his hot little hand in hers. 'I know, darling. But you'll soon feel better.' She looked back at the doctor with gratitude. 'Thank you so much for coming.'

'My pleasure,' he assured her. 'I'll look in on him again in the morning, if you like.'

'We would be very grateful,' said Rafael before Lauren could answer. 'You must allow me to escort you back to your room.'

Left alone with her sons, Lauren went and filled a bowl with warm water from the bathroom, and found a sponge. Nicolás was still sleeping the sleep of the just. Worn out from all the day's excitement. Lauren supposed. César complained peevishly as she sponged him, but there was no doubt that it cooled him. She allowed his skin to dry as per instructions, then repeated the process.

He was asleep by the time Rafael returned, the fever already reduced.

'I'm going to sit with him for a while,' she said. 'I want to be sure his temperature stays down.'

Rafael inclined his head in mute understanding. 'Would you like me to stay too?' he asked.

The urge to say yes was strong, but she doubted if the offer was seriously meant. 'There's no need for that,' she said. 'You may as well go to bed.' She hesitated briefly, avoiding his eyes. 'I'm sorry about... tonight.'

'There will be other nights.' He sounded dismissive. 'I'll leave you, then.'

He might at least have come and kissed her, she thought achingly as he went from the room. Love, not sex, that was what she needed right now. Only she wasn't going to get it, was she? Not from a man who saw her the way Rafael saw her. She stirred his loins, not his heart.

It was another hour or more before she felt able to steal away. César was sleeping a natural sleep, his skin so much cooler to the touch. The infection had been virulent while it lasted, but his basic good health had seen him through it. Hopefully there would be no after-effects.

Not until she reached her room and saw the empty bed did she acknowledge the faint hope that Rafael might have waited for her there. A ridiculous thought, anyway. As he had said, there were other nights. Even now, it wasn't his lovemaking she wanted so much as the simple comfort of his arms around her, and such forbearance on his part would have been most unlikely. That was something she had to accept.

As predicted, César showed no ill effects when he awakened. In fact, Lauren found, he didn't appear to remember anything of the night's activities. Advised of his patient's condition, Dr Manvers declared further examination unnecessary. He was glad to have been of service, he assured Lauren when she thanked him for his attention, even if only to reassure the anxious parent.

'I feel I should make some kind of gesture for his turning out in the middle of the night like that,' she said to Rafael after breakfast, when the boys had fled back upstairs to renew their acquaintance with new toys, 'but I'm not sure what. Offering a professional fee seems a bit crass.'

'He and his wife will be with us for a few more days yet,' Rafael replied casually. 'We'll invite them to dinner tomorrow evening.'

The 'we' warmed her—made her feel she belonged. 'A good idea,' she applauded.

'You must tell Juanita what you wish to be served,' he went on, bringing her down to earth again with a thump. 'From now, such matters will be your concern.'

'But I don't know any Spanish dishes,' Lauren protested. 'I wouldn't know where to start!'

'Then you must learn.' His tone was easy enough but with an underlying firmness. 'If you are to be mistress here, then you must act the part. Juanita speaks English. She will give you all the help you need.'

If she was to be mistress here? Was there, then, Lauren wondered, still some doubt in his mind? She knew a sudden drop in spirits at the idea. Yesterday he had seemed so adamant.

As if sensing her thoughts, he shook his head, a faint mockery in the line of his mouth. 'I meant only that there is more to being a wife than simply sharing my bed.'

'And more to life than glorified housekeeping,' she responded, taking refuge in sharpness. 'I'll never be the kind of wife content to accept *that* role!'

'We all have certain duties to perform,' he said. 'Were I demanding that you perform household tasks yourself, I could perhaps understand your reluctance.'

Lauren bit her lip. The rebuke was thoroughly deserved, she knew. 'I'm sorry,' she said in muted tones. 'I went over the top.'

'You feel honour-bound to stress your equality.' The comment was dry. 'If *I* can practise forbearance, is it too much to ask that you do so too?'

What forbearance? it was on the tip of her tongue to ask, but she bit it back. 'I'll try,' she said instead. 'Just don't expect miracles, that's all.' She sought a change of subject. 'Gabriel is late putting in an appearance this morning.'

Rafael's expression hardened. 'Gabriel has yet to return.'

'Oh?' She did her best to sound non-committal. 'Well, I suppose he found somewhere to stay.'

'No doubt.'

It was useless saying anything, Lauren decided wryly. Gabriel must fight his own battles. She had enough on her own plate.

'Wasn't it today that Isabella wanted the children to get together?' she asked.

The sidestep was accepted. 'Yes, it was. Isabella is the kind of friend you should cultivate for yourself.'

'With a view to learning how to become the ideal Spanish wife, you mean?' Lauren tried to keep the remark flippant.

'That,' he returned drily, 'would be asking too much. Isabella herself is no doormat—to use your own inelegant term—but she shows a proper respect for her husband's authority in the home. A clever woman uses strategy in her relationship with a man, and leaves his pride intact.'

'What about her own pride?' Lauren challenged, not about to let that pass. 'We're all of us entitled to it.'

'Not to the same degree. Pride is fundamental to the male psyche. Without it, he is but half a man.' Rafael was speaking lightly enough but with a look in his eyes that cautioned. 'Any man who allows a woman to better him is but half a man.'

Now, Lauren decided, was not the time to dispute that statement—at least, not openly. She stayed silent, holding his gaze with determination, seeing the spark give way to a mocking approval.

'There is hope yet,' he said. 'I look forward to your conversion.'

She had the sense not to answer that one either. Nothing she could say was going to alter his attitude; she would have to assert her independence by deed, not word. But only then where the situation really warranted it, came the mental rider. Opposing him on principle was verging on childishness.

The Caldas estate lay out towards Grazalema. Lauren was a little surprised to find a villa of modern design, although it blended quite well with its surroundings, she had to admit.

Isabella greeted them with pleasure, and took the four of them out to a spacious patio where Julio was playing ball with his daughter. Lauren fell for the curly-haired toddler on sight.

'She's lovely!' she exclaimed admiringly to Isabella as the twins joined in the game. 'So tiny, yet so perfect! Be gentle now,' she warned the boys.

Isabella laughed. 'Small though she is, she is very strong in spirit. Only the other day she pushed the five-year-old son of one of our friends into the swimming-pool when he tried to take something from her. He was immediately rescued, of course,' she added hastily. 'It would be foolish to leave small children to play unsupervised where there is water, do you not agree?'

'Of course.' Both César and Nicolás had swum from a very early age, but to say so, Lauren thought, might sound too self-congratulatory.

Inés lived up to her mother's boast by refusing to hand over the ball to César, choosing instead to present it to Nicolás, who looked first bemused and then gratified. For the first time ever, Lauren saw rivalry raise its head as César attempted to snatch the prize. Nicolás fended him off with equal ferocity.

'Enough!' said Rafael sharply. 'Nicolás, give the ball back to Inés.'

He obeyed at once, looking suddenly sheepish. The two boys stole sideways glances at each other, then broke into giggles, joined immediately by Inés herself.

'A trouble-maker,' commented Julio with wry humour.

Rafael smiled. 'But an irresistible one.'

'I thought you didn't care for spirit in the female of the species,' said Lauren in what was meant to be a jocular tone.

'Only where unbridled,' came the smooth reply. 'Inés will learn temperance from her mother.'

'One would trust,' said Julio, directing a fond glance at his wife. 'If not, she may have difficulty in finding a suitable husband when the time comes.'

'But you will allow her to make her own choice?' asked Lauren with deliberation, and heard Rafael's impatiently indrawn breath.

'Providing the choice was a good one,' Julio agreed. 'Perhaps one of your own sons, if you decide to stay.'

'Lauren and I are to marry,' declared Rafael before she could form any answer. 'So, yes, the possibility is very much there.'

If the Caldases were at all shocked by the news, they didn't show it. On the contrary, they both looked highly delighted.

'I am so happy for you!' exclaimed Isabella. 'When is the wedding to be?'

Recovering from her momentary suspension, Lauren opened her mouth to reply, only to have Rafael beat her to it again.

'As soon as it can be arranged. We have no reason to delay. Say one month from now.'

Whatever had to be said, Lauren decided, could hardly be said here and now with the Caldases present. Francisco had been dead only a few months. Under no circumstances would the wedding take place before the full year was out.

Rafael was looking at her with a quizzical expression as if waiting for some comment. She returned his gaze with a steadiness she was far from feeling, heart fluttering at the sheer impact of those dark eyes. It was a mistake to consider marrying him at all, knowing what she already knew of his nature. She was the one who would have to make all the concessions in the end. He was incapable of it.

Isabella insisted that they stay to lunch. Apart from a woman who came in to clean, and another who took care of the laundry, there were no servants in the household. Isabella did her own cooking, and did it beautifully.

Helping her clear away the dishes after the meal, Lauren found herself half wishing for the same comparatively simple lifestyle. Being waited on hand and foot was all very well for a while, but how long before it became tedious? The kitchens at Callahora were very much Juanita's province; she was hardly going to want *her* messing around when the fancy took her.

'Both Julio and I think very highly of Rafael,' Isabella declared as she loaded the dishwasher. 'He is a fine man, and will be a very good and responsible husband and father, I am sure. It is more than time for him to marry.'

'He must have had plenty of opportunity before this,' Lauren observed, adding with deliberation, 'Nina Ortega, for instance?'

'Nina Ortega is not the kind of woman he would have considered marrying!'

'But they have been . . . close.'

Isabella straightened, her expression uncomfortable. 'Men see such matters in a different light. She means nothing to him, I am sure.'

'You mean,' Lauren said with intent, 'that he simply used her?'

The discomfiture increased. 'Nina Ortega is a woman of the world. She cannot have imagined for a moment that there was any permanency in the arrangement.'

'Obviously there was no secret about it!'

'Not to any degree. Nina herself made little attempt to hide the fact. It was finished before you came, reluctant as she was to accept it.' Isabella hesitated before adding softly, 'What is past is past. You must look to the future.'

Right now, Lauren told herself wryly, she could do with a reliable crystal ball!

CHAPTER SEVEN

GABRIEL was still on the missing list when they returned to Callahora. Rafael said nothing when advised of the fact, but the narrowing of his lips spoke volumes for the kind of reception his brother was likely to suffer when he did eventually put in an appearance.

Those who live in glass houses, Lauren reflected with cynicism. If Gabriel had spent the night with a woman, he was doing no worse than Rafael himself had done. 'Men see such matters in a different light', Isabella had said, but only, it seemed, when applied to themselves.

'You had no right to tell the Caldases we were to be married in a month's time,' she accused when the two of them were alone. 'It's out of the question!'

'What reason would there be for waiting longer than that?' Rafael asked. 'Will you feel any differently in another few weeks or months?'

Lauren closed heart and mind to any messages from her senses. 'It just isn't decent to rush into it so soon, that's all.'

'In whose opinion? Your own, or that of others?'

'Both,' she claimed. 'Francisco might have had his faults, but he's entitled to some degree of respect.'

'You already devoted enough time to his memory,' came the reply. 'He merits no more. If not for yourself, then you should consider Nicolás's and César's welfare. They have need of a stabilising influence in their lives. One I can supply far better from within marriage than without.' He made a gesture signifying settlement of the question. 'We marry in one month. You may leave the arrangements to me. All that need concern you is your choice of dress—although white would, I think, be unsuitable in the circumstances. You agree?'

Lauren gazed at him indecisively, aware of a growing urge to give in and let him have his way. What difference could a few more months make in the end? He would still be the same man. It was all proving too much for her, she acknowledged. She didn't have the strength of mind to go on resisting him.

'I suppose not,' she heard herself saying. 'I can hardly claim to be a virgin.'

The firm mouth took on a slant. 'Virginity is as much a state of mind as of body. In many ways, you remain innocent.'

'Of what?' she asked. 'I made love with my husband's brother after knowing him less than two days. That scarcely makes me an innocent.'

'It scarcely makes you a scarlet woman either,' he responded drily. 'The time element is immaterial where two people share the same depth of desire. I saw the reflection of my own in your eyes the moment our fingers met that first evening when I handed you your glass. While I would naturally prefer to have been the first man to take you, I can at least be the last.'

Voice low, she said, 'Will the restriction apply equally to you too?'

One eyebrow lifted sardonically. 'Would you trust my word if I gave it?'

There was a pause before she answered. When she did speak it was with flat intonation. 'Probably not.'

'Then there is no point to my doing so.' He studied her for a moment, then rose suddenly from the chair where he was sitting and came over to draw her unresistingly to her feet. 'A woman has it in her power to be all things to a man,' he said softly.

The kiss was feather-light at first, a mere brushing movement that made her quiver like an aspen leaf. She could feel the heat of his hands burning through the thin material of her dress, the firm muscularity of his body as he drew her closer. Love in the afternoon, came the springing thought—better any day of the week than siesta!

'Come,' Rafael murmured. 'There are places more conducive than this.'

Lauren made no protest as he led her from the room. He pressed her ahead of him up the winding stairs, hands warm and possessive at her waist, urging her on when she attempted to stop at the first floor.

'The boys will be safe enough for another hour,' he said. 'They have plenty to occupy their attention if they waken.'

Lauren hoped he was right. The pair of them had certainly been tired enough to fall into an almost instant sleep on retiring to their beds half an hour ago. César in particular had some catching up to do, although he seemed to be suffering no after-effects from the infection itself.

Situated immediately above her own, Rafael's bedroom was furnished with heavily carved dark wood pieces and masculine austerity. He closed the door quietly and took her hand to turn her towards him as she stood irresolute, looking at the bed.

'You must make whatever changes you wish with the room when the time comes,' he said. 'A woman has more interest in such matters.'

Décor was the last thing on Lauren's mind at that moment. The blood drummed in her ears as he cupped her face between his hands to kiss her again, cherishing her lips in a way that melted her bones. She kissed him back feverishly, wantonly, seeking to lose herself in the sheer turmoil of emotion. Thinking was out; feeling was all that mattered at present. Wonderful, glorious sensation!

Stripped of his clothing, Rafael was magnificent; there was no other way to describe him. Tentative at first in her exploration of the tautly muscled body, she became increasingly bold and daring in realisation of the power she held in her hands. To hear his indrawn breath, to see the rictus in his face as she caressed him, to feel the pulsing life beneath her fingers was indescribable pleasure.

She had never wanted to do such things for Francisco; had never known what it was to take any initiative at all in lovemaking. With Rafael there were no limitations; she needed to know every inch of him, to kiss every inch of him, to give him more pleasure than *he* had ever known.

'*Alma de mi alma*,' he breathed. '*Flor de mi corazón*!'

Whatever that meant, the tone of it alone roused her to fever pitch. The time element had no bearing, he had said, and it hadn't, because she was in love with him—had been in love with him since the moment they had met. She could admit it at last.

The coming together was glorious. She wanted it to last for ever. Rafael controlled it as he controlled everything, bringing her to climax after climax before finally granting himself release. One day, she vowed, in the dreamy, satiated moments following, he would love her too, not just with his body but with his whole heart. She would *make* him love her!

'One month,' he said softly. 'No more,'

Next week wouldn't be too soon for her, thought Lauren recklessly. Rafael would be a husband in a million, a lover without equal, the kind of father her sons had never known and so needed.

'No more,' she repeated, and felt his chest expand to a slowly indrawn breath. Satisfaction, she wondered with a sudden and depressing return to uncertainty, or simply resignation? What did he stand to gain, after all, from the arrangement? A wife and ready-made family to support. Hardly the kind of circumstance he would have planned for himself. He was doing it only because he felt he owed it to his brother to take proper care of his sons. Had she been willing to turn them over to him, the marriage would have been unnecessary.

Finding her physically desirable was some small compensation, she supposed. But how long would that desire last without love to back it? How long before he became bored with her and sought other outlets for his masculine passions?

His movement away from her to sit up and reach for the silk robe draped across the nearby chair seemed to suggest that the boredom might already be setting in. Lauren watched him numbly as he crossed the room to what she took to be the bathroom door, hoping for some backward glance, some hint that he would be coming back to her. Only when the door had closed behind him did she force herself to accept that the session was over. Better all round if she were gone when he emerged again.

With no robe available, and hardly able to risk descending to her own floor stark naked, she hastily pulled on her dress and gathered the rest of her clothing. Hopefully, she could be showered and changed before the twins woke up. She refused to think any further ahead than that.

Nicolás and César were awake when she did look in on them some ten minutes later, but playing quite happily with the junior Monopoly set. They had found little difficulty in understanding the rules of the game once explained, and obviously enjoyed it. Capitalists in the making, Rafael had amusedly observed.

He had more time for the pair of them than Francisco had ever shown, Lauren conceded. On one momentous occasion, the latter had actually consented to take all three of them to the zoo, but had found the occasion so tedious that he had steered clear of family outings altogether after that. Whatever else might be lacking in this relationship, Rafael's regard for the boys came over loud and clear.

Was it possible, Lauren wondered wryly, to feel jealous of her own sons?

She sat with them while they ate supper, but took no more than a bite herself. Tomorrow, Elena would be here to supervise again, leaving her free to...do what? Rafael would more than likely be busy, Gabriel the same. She could always go for a walk, she supposed. The countryside certainly merited exploration.

At eight o'clock, with the twins bathed and bedded, if not yet asleep, she went to start preparing for dinner. She had seen nothing at all of Rafael since leaving his room, nor had Gabriel put in an appearance. Helpful and friendly as the staff were, they were no substitute for family companionship.

There was still no sign of Rafael when she went down to the *salón*, but Gabriel was there, glass in hand.

Not his first drink of the day, Lauren judged from the look of him. 'I was beginning to think you might have left home,' she said lightly.

'Or to hope?' he suggested on a sarcastic note.

'Why would I do that?'

He shrugged. 'I mean nothing to you.'

'That's nonsense,' she said. 'You're my brother-in-law. Of course you mean something to me!'

'As much as Rafael?' His lip curled as colour tinged her cheeks. 'Don't make the mistake of believing this marriage to be anything but what it is. From the very first moment he discovered the existence of Francisco's sons, he was determined to have them raised here under his influence, whatever it took. When my brother sets his mind to anything, he allows nothing to stand in his way!'

'I'm under no illusions,' she said, trying to keep her voice steady. 'I know exactly where I stand.'

'Then you are no better than he is!' The tone was scathing. 'All you look for is security.'

'There are worse things,' Lauren defended. 'I can't deny Nicolás and César the kind of future they'll have here, but neither can I give them up. It was Rafael's idea that we marry, not mine.' She made an appealing little gesture. 'Gabriel—Angel—I want us to be friends.'

His shrug dismissed the gesture. 'It's of little importance. I went to see Señor Flores today. Once Alicia and I are married, I'll be gone from Callahora for good.'

Lauren looked at him uncertainly. 'I thought you were totally against it?'

He smiled thinly. 'As you said yourself, there are worse things than a loveless marriage.'

Such as banishment from the only home he had ever known, she thought. So Rafael had already issued the ultimatum when he spoke of it last night, it seemed. There could be no other reason for such an abrupt about-face on Gabriel's part. It was cruel, and she would tell Rafael so! Not that it would do any good.

'I believe Alicia loves you, even if you don't feel the same way about her,' she said hesitantly, and saw Gabriel's lips curl.

'What would you know of her feelings? You met her only the once.'

She summoned a lighter tone. 'Call it feminine intuition.' Empathy would have been nearer the mark, but that was for her alone to know. She and Alicia had a lot in common—although she could at least find some solace in the physical expression of her emotions. Alicia would succumb to no such temptation outside of the marital bed, it was fairly certain.

'Did you really make the decision on your own?' she asked impulsively. 'Or are you simply giving in to pressure?'

He took his time answering, face reflecting a variety of expressions which eventually crystallised into resignation. 'I have no one else in mind.'

It was hardly an ideal basis, but then who was she to judge? Lauren asked herself.

'I'll look forward to meeting Alicia again,' she ventured. 'Soon, I hope?'

'You and she will be sisters-in-law before very long,' he said. He drained off the remaining alcohol in his glass in a single swallow, mouth twisting. 'One happy family!'

Rafael's arrival cut short the conversation, if that was what it could be called. He looked from her to his brother assessingly.

'I take it that the news has already been imparted?'

'Why keep it a secret?' asked Gabriel. 'We might even make it a double wedding!'

Rafael's expression darkened. 'A joke in poor taste.'

The younger man shrugged. 'You're right, of course—as you always are.'

The sarcasm was ignored. Not worth getting angry about, Lauren gathered. Gabriel had upheld the family honour; that was all Rafael considered important. As Gabriel had said, he was utterly without scruples when it came to getting his way.

Gabriel had little to say all through dinner. Lauren gave up trying after receiving monosyllabic replies to her overtures. He might have reconciled himself to this marriage, but he still wasn't happy about it, that was apparent.

She was far from happy herself, if it came to that. Rafael's whole attitude towards her seemed so cool and impersonal. It was difficult to believe that this was the same man who had made such passionate love to her a few short hours ago.

But then, why should he bother making any further effort to charm when he already had what he wanted from her? She had proved an absolute walkover, hadn't she? Small wonder that he was bored with her already. Once they were married he might even dispense with her services altogether. Why bother, when he could find so much more enticement elsewhere? Nina Ortega, for instance. Had he ever really intended giving her up, or had she simply been shelved for some future date?

Her spirit suddenly reasserted itself. She wasn't married to him yet; it wasn't too late to back out of the arrangement. Accepting his word that a Spanish court would automatically award him custody of her sons had been foolish to start with. They were British. No court could totally ignore that fact.

What she felt for him wasn't love, she told herself fiercely, it was simple and shameful lust! She had been mesmerised by it, but no more. From this moment on, she was her own person again!

As if sensing some change in her, he gave her a narrowed glance. Lauren returned it without a flicker, closing heart and mind to the sensual stirring he could even now rouse in her. Nothing he could either do or say was going to undermine her resolve this time. The whole idea had been ridiculous from the start!

He made no attempt to delay her when she announced her intention of retiring soon after the meal was finished. She looked in on the twins before going to her room, relieved to find the two of them sound asleep. They belonged to her, no one else. She would do whatever was necessary to retain them.

Regardless of what he might or might not feel, there was a chance that Rafael would still visit her. She locked the door against the possibility, and lay awake for a long time waiting, but he didn't come.

When she did sleep it was fitfully. She rose at seven feeling anything but refreshed, but with no waning of determination. At the very first opportunity she would make it clear that the marriage was off and would stay off. What happened after that would depend on Rafael himself, although it was doubtful if he would simply give in and allow the three of them to leave. But, whatever the fight ahead, he wasn't going to win.

Contrary to Gabriel's intimation that his brother always took breakfast early during the week, the latter was seated at table when she went in to breakfast. His greeting was easy enough, but there was something in the dark eyes that gave the lie to his apparent good humour. From the look of him, Gabriel hadn't slept very well either.

'I forgot to mention last night that the Floreses expect us to dine this evening,' he said tonelessly.

Rafael nodded. 'In which case, I'll ask the Manverses to dine with us the following evening.'

Lauren had forgotten about that. Entertaining Dr Manvers and his wife was a small enough return for the attention given her son, reluctant though she was to act hostess to Rafael's host. As he would know by then of her decision to withdraw from their arrangement, it was unlikely to prove a relaxing occasion. They would both of them have to be on their guard to show an agreeable front.

Eager to initiate Elena into the intricacies of Monopoly, the twins could hardly wait to leave the table. Lauren tried not to mind too much. As their mother, she held a special place in their hearts, and hopefully always would. Their affection for others was in no way a threat.

But what of their feelings towards Rafael himself? How were they going to react when she told them of her change of heart? They saw him with different eyes. How could they be expected to understand? She would be depriving them of the father figure so eagerly accepted—tearing them away from their new home. And if Rafael did by some chance manage to win custody, what then? Could she face the prospect of returning to England without them?

It wouldn't come to that, she told herself forcefully. As to the rest, she would deal with it as and when. If a daddy was what Nicolás and César wanted most in the world, then she would provide them with one. Only not Rafael!

'I have to visit Estepona this morning,' he said, breaking in on her thoughts. 'I thought you might like to accompany me?'

Right now the last thing she wanted was to be on her own with him, but the sooner she got things straightened out the better, she supposed. The rest of the things they had purchased on Saturday would be arriving this morning, so the boys would be fully occupied.

'Thank you,' she said formally. 'That would be...nice.'

If he noted her slight hesitation over the word, he gave no sign of it. 'Be ready to leave in half an hour,' he said, getting to his feet.

'You and Alicia will have a lot to talk about tonight,' observed Gabriel with sardonic inflexion, helping himself to more coffee as his brother left the room. 'She was delighted to hear that you and Rafael were to marry too.'

'I hadn't realised I was invited,' Lauren confessed, and saw his brows lift.

'Why would my brother's intended not be included? It's true that the news caused some surprise, considering the short time that you've been here with us, but no one is likely to question Rafael's judgement. He was always a law unto himself.'

'I'm sure!' The bitter comment was out before she could stop it, eliciting a sudden spark in Gabriel's eyes.

'So you begin to have doubts about this marriage after all?'

'Don't read too much into too little,' she hedged. 'I'm not in any doubt.'

'Then you really intend to go through with it?'

The lie came too hard; she settled for prevarication again. 'Why not?'

'A question answered by another usually suggests evasion,' he said. 'I think you may be having second thoughts.'

Unable to deny it, she sought refuge in anger. 'I think *you* should confine yourself to your own affairs!'

An unwilling smile touched his mouth as he studied her. 'If Alicia had even a small amount of your spirit!'

Lauren eyed him back in sudden speculation, temporarily sidetracked. 'Would that make her more attractive to you?'

'It might make her less tedious,' he conceded.

'That's a horrible way to talk about her!' she protested. '*I* didn't find her tedious the other evening. We talked about all kinds of things.'

'And she agreed with you on everything, of course.'

She hesitated, knowing he was right yet reluctant to admit it. 'Well...yes, I suppose so. But she was only being polite.'

'She was being what she's been taught to be,' he said. 'She has no mind of her own.'

'Then tell her she's free to have opinions so far as you're concerned, if that's what you really want. A lot of men would be only too pleased to have a wife who agreed with their every word!'

'Such as my brother?' Gabriel suggested slyly, and smiled again when she failed to answer. 'In that case, you're far from right for him—or he for you, for that matter. Can you seriously contemplate spending your life with a man who would think nothing of beating you if you provoked his anger too far?'

It might just be true, Lauren reflected. Not that it mattered any more, anyway.

'I think I'd better go and get ready,' she said shortly. 'You go too far yourself.'

'Because I tell you the truth?' He shook his head. 'Close your eyes to it if you will, but you will see that I'm right in the end.'

She left him sitting there, anxious to get away before she finished up acknowledging her change of heart. Rafael had to be the first to hear it. That was only just.

Wearing a lightweight suit in pale beige, he was waiting for her by the car when she got outside. His eyes held an unreadable expression as he viewed her own choice of green pleated skirt and sleeveless top.

'I hope this is suitable,' she said. 'It was so warm down at the coast on Saturday.'

'Quite suitable,' Rafael confirmed. 'Your taste is excellent.'

He saw her into her seat before coming round to slide his length behind the wheel. Seen in profile, his face looked austere. Was he perhaps having second thoughts himself? Lauren wondered. Had he finally begun to realise just how impossible the marriage would be? The question of the twins' future would still remain, but some kind of compromise could surely be reached.

Such as what? came the dispiriting thought. Whatever his views on their own relationship, he was unlikely to make any concessions where the twins themselves were concerned. It would simply be back to square one.

They had been driving for some time before she nerved herself to set the ball rolling. There was little point, she decided at length, in waiting for an opportune moment. She had to get it over with.

Her voice sounded husky when she finally said the words. 'I'm not going to marry you, Rafael.'

From the corner of her eye, she saw his knuckles whiten as if his hands had momentarily tensed on the wheel.

'Is that so?' he said.

The tone alone was enough to make her heart jerk. He hadn't changed *his* mind, it was obvious. No doubt he regarded vacillation of any kind a sign of weakness.

'It isn't going to work,' she appealed. 'You have to see that. It simply isn't going to work!'

'What would you consider is missing?' he asked. 'Are you trying to say that you feel nothing when we're together?'

She drew in a shaky breath. 'There are more important factors.'

'So tell me,' he invited.

'Love, for instance,' she burst out. 'I realise it's unimportant to you, but it isn't to me.'

Rafael kept his gaze on the road ahead, his expression neutral. 'You married my brother without it.'

'Not knowingly. I really believed I was in love with him. In any case——' She broke off, catching her lower lip between her teeth.

'In any case, there was your pregnancy to consider,' he finished for her. 'Does the same not apply where your sons are concerned?'

'It's a totally different thing.'

'In the sense that they themselves are in a position to make their wishes known, I would agree. You allowed them to believe that I'm to be their *papá*. Would you break your word to them?'

'It's my life too!' she claimed forcefully.

'And what exactly are you being asked to sacrifice? A few romantic notions, no more!' His tone was hard. 'Many women would consider themselves well recompensed.'

'Then marry one of *them*!' she flashed. 'Nina Ortega, perhaps? I'm sure she can give you far greater satisfaction than I can!'

They were coming up to a railed-off viewpoint overlooking the valley far below. Rafael turned in with a crunching of gravel to bring the car to a jerky halt. The gaze he turned on her was penetrating.

'In what way do you think me dissatisfied?'

'You know very well what I'm talking about,' she mumbled.

'You mean sexually?'

Colour stained her cheeks. 'I don't intend even attempting to compete with the women you've known before.'

'If that kind of expertise was all I looked for in a wife, I'd be married already,' he said drily. 'Do you imagine me capable of faking my physiological responses when we make love?'

The flush deepened. 'No, of course not.'

'Then you must be aware of the pleasure you give me.' He put out a hand and turned her face towards him, forcing her to look at him directly. There was a deep-down spark in the darkness of his eyes. 'A pleasure I have no intention of giving up. You belong to me, Lauren. You will always belong to me!'

'You can't own someone,' she whispered, already hovering on the brink of surrender. 'I belong to myself.'

'Then I'll own a part of you,' he declared. 'This part!'

His lips were possessive, the hand seeking her breast equally so. She struggled against him for only a moment before giving way to the emotions he could so easily conjure in her. Whether it was love or not, she didn't know and scarcely cared. It was enough for the moment just to feel.

She kept her eyes closed against his scrutiny when he lifted his head at last, reluctant to let him see the extent of her capitulation. He wasn't bored with her; how could she have thought it? His desire for her was just as great.

'So it was only my failure to convey satisfaction that drove you away so abruptly yesterday,' he said softly. 'I must take better care in future.'

If she were to dispute the matter any further, it had to be here and now, Lauren knew, but she couldn't find it in herself to do it. They would just have to make the best they could of this marriage. Love could grow along with a better knowledge of one another. And if it didn't, well, they'd have to do without. Others managed it.

He gave her cheek a final caress before turning back to switch on the ignition once more. Her boats were well and truly burned this time, thought Lauren fatalistically as he set the car into motion, yet she couldn't feel any real regret. There were far worse ways to live, far worse men to live with—as she knew to her cost. She should consider herself fortunate to have this much.

CHAPTER EIGHT

THE hotel San Nicolás lay on the coastal road just outside the town. Like the one in Marbella, it had an air of exclusivity. Not open to the package operators, Rafael confirmed. The third and last of the Quiros chain in Torremolinos covered that end of the market.

'The clientele here is largely Spanish and German,' he said as he drew the car to a halt in the car park. 'Only the occasional English party. You might like to take coffee on the terrace while I meet with the management. It should take no more than an hour to conclude business affairs, then we'll visit the harbour.'

Lauren would have much preferred to attend the meeting herself, but he was hardly likely to agree to that. Business matters were his province; she could almost hear him saying it.

'Fine,' she agreed. 'I'll look forward to it.'

The well-dressed and fortyish manager greeted his employer with an obsequiousness that set Lauren's teeth on edge. The man must be good at his job or he wouldn't be here, so the fawning was surely unnecessary. Unless she completely misjudged him, it seemed unlikely that Rafael himself would expect it.

From the rear of the hotel, a series of broad terraces dropped to the sea-shore, the slopes between landscaped into a tropical garden with a multitude of palms and flowering shrubs. The uppermost terrace was set out with tables and chairs already well occupied by those taking mid-morning refreshment.

Seated on her own by a tinkling waterfall, with the sun so beautifully warm on her face, Lauren felt quite happy to linger. The coffee was excellent, the ambience wonderful, the weather perfect. A companion to share it with was all that was missing, but one couldn't have everything. Rafael would be here soon enough.

She thought at first that it was the waiter returning when someone paused at her table. Looking up to meet Xaviour Ríos's boldly speculative gaze was something of a shock.

'You are all alone?' he asked.

Lauren smiled and shook her head. 'Rafael is in a meeting with the management. He'll be joining me shortly.' She added lightly, 'What are you doing here?'

'Meeting with friends who are staying in the hotel,' he returned. 'The arrangement was to see them here on the terrace at eleven, but it's now fifteen minutes past the hour, and they have still to appear. I was about to go and find them when I saw you sitting here. A beautiful woman should never be left alone!'

'Well, I shan't be for much longer,' she said, disregarding the fulsome compliment. 'As I told you, Rafael will be joining me soon.' It was going to be at least another half an hour before he did so, but that was beside the point. Knowing how he felt about the man, Lauren decided that Xaviour Ríos was the last person she wanted around when he did come to find her.

Xaviour, it appeared, took little heed of hints. Either that, or it didn't occur to him that his company might be unwelcome. 'Then I'll join you until he arrives,' he said, pulling out a chair. 'You would like more coffee? Or something a little stronger, perhaps?'

Short of being very blunt, there was no way she was going to get rid of him, Lauren acknowledged wryly.

She would have to make the best of it. 'Nothing for me, thanks,' she said. 'I've had enough already.'

'Then I too will abstain.' He treated her to a slow sensual smile. 'It's refreshment enough to sit and look at you—to drink in your beauty with eyes dazzled by the gold in your hair. You stir me more than any other woman I know, *querida*!'

'Even Nina Ortega?' she asked on a bland note.

If he recognised the mockery he didn't reveal it. 'I have no interest in Nina Ortega,' he declared. 'Not since I first saw you. She is all Rafael's.'

'That's all over!' she said sharply, and saw his eyes narrow a fraction as if in sudden comprehension.

'If that is what he tells you, he is lying. He warned me himself to stay away from her. Not that I would have taken any heed,' he hastened to add, 'had I not already decided it for myself. I intended to telephone you in a day or two and suggest that we spend an evening together, but now I have no need. When will be convenient for you?'

He was the one lying! Lauren told herself numbly, and knew she didn't really believe it. He had no reason to lie. If Rafael was possessive over the woman, it could only be because he still wanted her himself.

So what if he did? she tried to reason. A man might desire many women without necessarily indulging the need. It would be up to her to keep him satisfied.

'I asked which evening you would like to come out with me?' Xaviour sounded a little put out.

Lauren summoned a smile, a gesture of polite regret. 'I'm afraid that won't be possible. You see, Rafael and I are to be married.'

He gazed at her in startled silence for a moment. 'But you have only been here in Spain a few days,' he said at length.

'It happens that way sometimes.' She did her best to sound buoyant. 'A few days, a few weeks, what does it matter?'

'I congratulate you.' There was irony now in his voice. 'It appears that Nina was right after all in doubting your innocence.'

'If you're suggesting that I came here intending this to happen, then you're wrong!' she flashed. 'You obviously don't know Rafael very well at all if you imagine for a moment that he'd allow himself to be manipulated by *any* woman!'

'You are the mother of his brother's sons,' Xaviour responded. 'His safeguard, perhaps, against having no son of his own to inherit the Quiros estates. What will happen to *them*, I wonder, if you give him a son?'

Lauren bit back her instinctive answer. 'That's hardly your concern. In fact, none of it is! And I'd prefer to be alone, if you don't mind.'

'By all means.' He came smoothly to his feet, pausing to look down at her with a sneer. 'I envy Rafael the pleasure of your body, *querida*.'

He was gone before she could draw breath to protest. Not that it would have made any difference, anyway. The man was too thick-skinned to be reached by words alone. She felt sullied by his contempt, yet at the same time half deserving of it. She should have had the strength of mind to stick to her guns earlier.

She was sitting watching the bathers in the pool below when Rafael came to find her.

'I understand you were joined by some man a short time ago,' he said without preamble. 'Who was he?'

'Do your minions spy on all your guests as a matter of course,' Lauren snapped back, 'or was this a one-off?'

He took a seat opposite, expression set. 'I left instructions that you were to be afforded every attention. Naturally a watch was kept on you. I repeat, who was he?'

'Xaviour Ríos.' The name came jerkily. 'He was supposed to be meeting friends who are staying here, but they hadn't turned up. He was simply passing the time of day.'

'That I doubt. Ríos wastes no time on such niceties.' He paused, face unrelenting. 'What did he say to you?'

Why prevaricate? Lauren asked herself. She hadn't offered the man any encouragement. 'He asked to take me out one evening.'

The dark eyes acquired a new spark. 'And you told him what?'

She looked back at him steadily. 'I told him it wouldn't be possible as you and I were to be married.'

'But you would have accepted had we not?'

Resentment at the inquisition drew the lie to her lips. 'I might have. He's an attractive man.' She added with intent, 'Nina Ortega seems to find him an acceptable replacement.'

Rafael's lips tautened ominously. 'That is another matter. As my *novia*, you invite *no* other man to sit with you!'

'I didn't invite him,' she denied. 'How was I supposed to stop him?'

'By telling him plainly that you had no wish for his company.'

'I doubt if he'd have taken any notice.' Lauren was struggling to retain a hold on her temper. 'And, while we're on the subject, I'm capable of deciding for myself whom I should or shouldn't speak with! You don't own me!'

The spark had become a glitter, dangerous in its intensity. 'We shall see about that.'

'No, we won't!' She was trembling, though not with fear. 'I'm not subjugating myself to any of your tin-pot rules on how I should behave. If that's your idea of marriage, you can keep it!'

Her voice had risen over the last few words, drawing attention from those parties near by. Rafael paid them no heed. His attention was concentrated solely on her.

'I don't ask for your subjugation,' he said, 'only for your restraint. Am I to be threatened with a withdrawal from our betrothal every time I say or do something you don't care for?'

Anger subsiding, Lauren made a helpless little gesture. 'I can't ever be the kind of woman you want me to be,' she said, low-toned. 'All it's going to mean is friction.'

It was a moment or two before he answered, expression difficult now to read. 'Then we have to find a degree of compromise,' he said at length. 'For Nicolás's and César's sake, if not for our own. They have need of a harmonious environment.'

Lauren could agree with that much. They'd never known what it was to have a proper family relationship. 'You don't know how to compromise,' she returned pessimistically, and saw a dry smile touch his lips.

'In that way, I think we may be two of a kind. So we must both of us learn. For now, I'd suggest that we concentrate on enjoying the rest of the day.' The smile flickered again. 'Agreed?'

It was something, Lauren supposed, that he could find humour in the situation, forced though it might well be. If he were willing to give it a go then she could surely do no less. She conjured a smile of her own, trying not to heed the doubts still there in her mind. 'Agreed.'

The harbour proved one of the most picturesque she had seen. Rafael walked her out along the sea wall for an overall view of the waterfront and town, backed by the lofting heights of the Sierra Bermeja. Early in the season though it was, the heat was already shimmering the distances. Come midsummer, Lauren reckoned, it would be in the nineties at this hour of the day.

They spent a lazy and surprisingly congenial two hours over lunch at one of the harbour restaurants, before heading back along the coast to San Pedro and the Ronda road. Familiarity was beginning to lessen the impact of the dizzy bends, Lauren found. Rafael probably had a point in saying that her acrophobia would give way to a gradual desensitisation. All the same, she had no intention of ever venturing on to the roof again.

The atmosphere between them was much more relaxed: no further reference had been made to the morning's contretemps. If Rafael could put Xaviour Ríos from mind, then so could she—including his intimations regarding Nina Ortega. From now on, she must place her trust in Rafael's word, not that of a man she had no feeling for whatsoever.

She was surprised but not displeased when he elected to come with her to find the twins on their arrival at the castle. They were in their room, along with Elena and Gabriel. Between them, they had fixed up the train-set on its trestle-table and were playing like four children together.

'I had to test it,' said Gabriel a little sheepishly. 'To make sure the electrics were safe.'

'A commendable notion,' agreed his brother, straight-faced.

'I'm the station master,' announced César proudly. 'And Nico's the guard. Uncle Gabriel is chief engineer, and Elena looks after the passengers.'

'I am afraid that the afternoon rest was forgotten,' confessed the girl, looking uncomfortable in her employer's presence. 'It will not happen again.'

'It won't do any harm for once,' said Lauren before Rafael could speak. 'I doubt if it would have been possible, anyway, with all this going on.' She looked round at the various items scattered about the room, wondering where they were going to find cupboard space to store it all. The junior drum kit was a worry of a different kind.

'The walls are too thick for sound to penetrate very far,' Rafael assured her, accurately guessing her thoughts. 'And the guest quarters, in any case, are too far away.'

'Come and play trains,' urged César, and was instantly backed by his brother.

Their uncle glanced at the gold watch spanning one lean wrist, and smiled. 'Why not?'

On the grounds that space about the table was limited, Lauren elected to stand and watch along with Elena, enjoying the spectacle of two grown men becoming boys again. That Rafael could bring himself down to their level without showing the least sign of reticence was heart-warming. Francisco would have died rather than do the same.

Elena herself seemed utterly bemused by her employer's metamorphosis. Don Rafael on his knees playing trains; who was going to believe it?

His regret seemed entirely genuine when he finally called a halt. 'I have to go now,' he said to the boys, 'but I'd very much like to join you again another day.'

He added to Gabriel, 'We must leave no later than eight-thirty.'

Lauren had forgotten until then about dining with the Floreses. So, it appeared from the sudden fading of animation from his face, had Gabriel. It was only a little after four-thirty now. What, she wondered, did Rafael have to do that necessitated his leaving so soon? Not business at this hour, surely?

'Shall we see you before then?' she asked lightly when he looked her way. 'Or are you going to be tied up for the rest of the afternoon?'

'It depends on how quickly I do what I have to do,' came the easy if unenlightening reply. 'In the meantime, you may take my place as head porter.'

'It is time too for me to leave,' said Elena as he went from the room. 'I will return at eight o'clock.'

Rafael would have arranged for her to baby-sit while they were out, Lauren assumed. If the evening extended into the small hours, as seemed normal here, it was going to be a long day for her.

'You must take the day off tomorrow,' she said. 'I'll be here to look after the children.'

The girl looked nonplussed. 'Don Rafael said nothing of this,' she murmured hesitantly. 'He gave me to understand that my services would be required each day. I very much enjoy being with Nicolás and César, *señora*. I hope I have done nothing wrong?'

The boys and their remaining uncle were involved once more in their improvised time-table, and taking little apparent note of the conversation. Lauren gave the Spanish girl a reassuring smile.

'Of course not. I thought you might like to sleep in a little later than usual, that's all.'

'I rise always at six, *señora*,' came the firm response. 'I would not wish Don Rafael to think I neglect my duties.'

Lauren gave up. It would upset the girl too much to insist on her staying away, much as she herself would have appreciated a whole day on her own with the twins. For all she knew, Rafael had something planned, anyway. He was unlikely to consult her first.

'It's your orders she should be obeying, not Rafael's,' observed Gabriel unexpectedly after Elena had departed.

'But it's Rafael she's employed by,' Lauren pointed out. 'I can hardly blame her for seeing it that way.'

'And you're willing to accept it?' Gabriel had moved away from the table now, leaving the two boys to play alone. 'I thought you were more independent than that.'

'Only where it comes to matters of real importance,' she rejoined determinedly. 'The twins benefit from Elena's being here. She's teaching them to speak Spanish, for one thing. Come the end of the summer, when they're due to start school, that will be a great advantage.'

'Rafael intends to arrange for private tutorage to begin with,' Gabriel advised, and lifted a mocking eyebrow as her expression altered. 'He didn't tell you?'

She kept her tone level. 'I believe he did mention it once, but only as a suggestion. When did he talk to you about it?'

'When he learned of their advanced intelligence. He already has someone in mind for the post.'

'Has he, though?' This time Lauren was unable to conceal the anger rising in her. She lightened her tone with an effort to add to the twins, 'It's almost supper time. You'd better start thinking about washing your hands.'

'We're not dirty,' Nicolás protested.

'We could have supper here,' chimed in César, 'then we don't need to wash at all.'

If Rafael were here there would be no argument, Lauren suspected. His authority was in no doubt. The thought alone goaded her beyond endurance. 'I'm sick and tired of the two of you cheeking me!' she snapped. 'Go and wash your hands. Now!'

They had heard her raise her voice to them before, but never with quite such vehemence. Eyes widened, faces registering confusion, they stared at her without moving for a long moment. Lauren hardened her heart against the urge to run and scoop them up, to cover them with reassuring, apologetic kisses. It was time they realised just who was in charge!

All the same, she felt like some wicked stepmother when the two of them went without further telling to do as they were bid. They were only four years old, for heaven's sake! How could she have been so nasty with them?

'I feel awful,' she confessed to Gabriel. 'I've never shouted at them like that before.'

'They were disobedient,' he said. 'You had reason to be cross.'

'But not vicious with it.' She made a helpless little gesture. 'I don't know what came over me.'

'My brother caused you to lose your temper,' he declared, conveniently ignoring the fact that he was as much to blame for telling her in the first place. 'He has no right to arrange matters without your agreement.'

Especially before the question of her staying here on a permanent basis had even been decided. Lauren knew a powerful urge to go after him right now and face him with it.

Except that three days ago the word compromise hadn't been mooted either, she reminded herself, trying to be rational about it. Angry accusations on her part were the last thing needed if they were ever to reach a unified understanding. She should wait for the right moment rather than rush in like a bull at a gate.

'I'll speak to him about it later,' she said dismissively.

The twins were a little subdued at supper, although Lauren made every effort to dispel any lingering after-effects of her outburst. They were normal, sometimes naughty, sometimes defiant little boys, not unruly terrors. Telling them she was sick of them was shameful. It was only natural that they would take more notice of Rafael, not just because he was male, but because he was still an unknown quantity.

Tucking them into bed later, she whispered, 'I love you,' before kissing each small forehead, and was rewarded with a hug and a look of relief from them both. It took so little to destroy a child's trust; a word of rejection spoken in anger could hurt far more than a smack. Never again, she vowed. No matter how disobedient they were, she would bite off her tongue before allowing it to run away with her to that extent.

They were asleep when Elena returned. Lauren was perturbed to realise that the girl was proposing to spend the whole evening seated on the couch outside their door where she would be on hand if her charges awoke.

'There's no need for that,' she assured her. 'If they do waken up, they have plenty to entertain themselves with.'

'I must be near should they need anything,' the other insisted. 'Don Rafael instructed that I keep a close watch.'

In case they took advantage of his absence to forget the ban he had imposed, Lauren surmised.

'Supposing you sit in my room?' she suggested. 'There are plenty of magazines and books, and if you leave the door open you'll be able to hear and see if they do leave their room.'

Elena hesitated. 'It would not be proper.'

'It would only be improper if you did it without my permission,' Lauren returned briskly. 'I've finished getting ready, so you can make yourself comfortable right away.'

There was a shy admiration in the girl's eyes as she appraised the dark blue silk tunic falling in narrow pleats from neckline to hem. 'You look very beautiful, *señora*. I hope you and Don Rafael will be very happy.'

So the news was already out. Leaked by Rafael himself, Lauren wondered, or Gabriel? Not that it made any difference.

'Thank you,' she said. 'I'm sure we shall be.'

Saying it didn't make it certain, though, came the wry thought. They had a long way to go to achieve even moderate harmony.

Resigned, if only on the surface, to his fate, Gabriel put on a surprisingly good face for the evening. The Floreses were eager to have the wedding date set, and preparations begun. Afraid, perhaps, that their future son-in-law might still back out, thought Lauren. She didn't believe there was much chance of that herself. Not after giving his word on it.

Alicia said little, but she looked as if a lamp had been lit inside her. There was no doubt at all that she worshipped the ground Gabriel walked on. That was probably half the trouble, Lauren conjectured. There had never been any challenge.

Because of her happiness, the younger girl looked prettier tonight, but her hair was still scraped back from her face in the severe and ageing fashion also favoured by her mother. Loosened, and allowed to fall naturally, it would be so much more flattering. Lauren wondered if she dared suggest it some time. It would be nice if she and Alicia could become friends as well as sisters-in-law.

Clad in formal grey, with shirt sparkling white against olive skin, Rafael was deep in discussion with Señor Flores. By this time next month, if he had his way, he would be her husband. Better if they got it out of the way before Gabriel and Alicia's big day, she had to concede. They had been allowed six weeks in which to prepare themselves.

As if sensing her regard, Rafael glanced across at her and smiled, and her heart flipped over. It was so easy for him. He didn't know what it was to have doubts. He didn't know what it was to love either. Not in any meaningful sense. Like Francisco before him, he saw it as synonymous with sex. At least they had more going for them in that direction than she had had with Francisco.

With or without love, she wanted him, she thought in sudden overriding hunger. Tonight, tomorrow—whenever! It seemed a lifetime since he had held her in his arms, those powerful, possessive arms she longed to feel again. A lot of women would envy her that opportunity alone.

Gabriel was summoned to join the other two men, leaving Alicia alone for the moment. On impulse, Lauren went to take the vacated seat, smiling at the younger girl.

'If we're to be sisters, we should start getting to know one another,' she said. 'Perhaps we could meet for coffee or something in Ronda tomorrow? I've only visited the town once since I've been here. It would be nice to take a look around the shopping areas.'

'It is mostly for the tourist at this time of the year,' returned the other with the same appealing diffidence Elena displayed, 'but I would very much like it if you came here to take coffee.'

Lauren was quick to recognise a gaffe; girls of Alicia's social strata obviously didn't meet up in coffee bars.

'I'd love to,' she said. 'I'll borrow a car and drive myself over. About what time?'

'Whenever you choose.' Alicia looked at her with interest and not a little envy. 'I would like to learn to drive a car, but *Padre* thinks not.'

'He's probably thinking of your safety,' said Lauren diplomatically. 'Perhaps Gabriel will teach you after you're married.'

The big dark eyes which were her one real claim to beauty widened still further. 'Gabriel?'

'Why not. It would make life easier for you both if you could get around without having to wait for him to accompany you.' Lauren added casually, 'He admires women who are independent. He told me so.'

'You, perhaps. You are English.'

'What difference does that make?'

Alicia gave a brief smile. 'You do not understand our ways.'

'But I understand the man you're to marry,' Lauren came back daringly. 'He wants a wife who can think for herself—give an opinion—make decisions. If you want to make him really happy, you'll have to stop agreeing with him all the time and say what you really think. Believe me, he'll appreciate it.'

To judge from her expression, Alicia didn't believe a word of it. 'I will think about what you say,' she promised politely.

And that, Lauren judged, was probably as far as she was going to get. It would be up to Gabriel himself to penetrate that shell of reserve—if he wanted to.

She insisted on the two men sitting together up front on their return to Callahora, content herself to sink into the comfortable soft leather of the shaped rear seat and feast her eyes on Rafael's profile outlined by starlight.

Tonight, she would kiss those firm lips, caress the smoothly muscled, superbly toned body, feel the surging power in his loins as he took her to him. The excitement of it was like fire in her veins. Had they been alone, she would have asked him to stop the car and make love to her right here and now. Two of a kind, he had called them. In more ways than the one, it seemed.

The evening had not been as prolonged as she had anticipated, but it was still close to one o'clock when they reached the castle. Gabriel said an immediate goodnight and departed for his own quarters.

'I think it time we too retired,' said Rafael softly. His hand was warm at her back, urging her in the direction of the tower steps. 'We have much to make up for.'

It was only when she reached the landing and saw the open door that Lauren remembered Elena. Rafael must have forgotten about her too.

'I gave Elena permission to sit in my room,' she whispered, coming to an abrupt halt.

'Then we will go to my room,' he said.

'That's hardly possible.' The denial was dragged from her. 'I can't just leave her there.'

'No, perhaps not.' There was regret in his voice, but no more. 'We must say goodnight, then.'

The kiss was quick and light—too light. 'What do I do with her?' Lauren asked as he began to turn away, unable to believe he was just going to accept the deprivation of a night together.

'She is to spend the night in the staff quarters,' he said. 'She knows the way.'

Still more than half anticipating some intimation that he would return after she dispatched the Spanish girl, Lauren watched him out of sight around the curve of the staircase before forcing herself into movement. If he could so easily forgo making love to her, he couldn't want her all *that* badly, she thought with a swift return to depression.

She found Elena wide awake and somewhat reluctant to report that she had caught the twins out of their room some time earlier.

'They were thirsty,' she explained, 'and were making their way to the kitchens to find drinks. I brought orange juice for them, and they returned to sleep.'

The kitchens, Lauren wondered, or the roof? She had thought it unlikely that they'd venture up there again after Rafael's stern edict, but children had short memories. They could fib with the best when it suited, *and* look like angels while doing it.

She went in to look at the pair of them after Elena had departed. As the girl had said, they were asleep once more, innocence written large on each smooth, olive-skinned face. They looked wholly Spanish, Lauren was bound to admit. No one would ever take them for her sons. Not that she would change a hair on their heads.

It was doubtful if they would waken again before morning, but she left her door ajar just in case. Years of motherhood had sharpened her hearing to a point where any untoward sound would bring her out of the deepest sleep. Tomorrow, she would ask Rafael if the door giving access to the roof could be locked; that would be the best way of ensuring no further exploratory trips—in that direction at least.

Sleep was a long time coming, and had lasted what seemed like bare moments when she was jerked from it by some movement in the room.

'What are you doing?' she asked sharply, sitting up. 'You should be in bed!'

'That is the intention,' said Rafael on an amused note as he pulled back the cover to slide in beside her. 'Did you believe I could endure the night without you?'

Happiness swelled her heart and she opened her arms to him, drawing him close where she could feel every hard and vital line of him. He had shed whatever garments he had been wearing, and was naked, skin warm and dry, body hair electric even through the filmy material of her nightdress.

'You have no need of this,' he said, and peeled the garment from her, flinging back the covers at the same time so that he could see her in entirety.

Lauren felt her breath catch in her throat and her knees turn to jelly as he ran a proprietorial hand down the full length of her body. She was ready to do anything he wanted, *be* anything he wanted, just so long as he went on wanting her.

Stopping herself from saying the words was the most difficult thing she had ever done. It wasn't her love he desired, only her body. But there was no reason why she couldn't hope, was there?

CHAPTER NINE

THE pillow at her side was empty when Lauren awoke. Rafael would have returned to his own room before first light in case the boys discovered them, she surmised, although she couldn't recall his leaving.

She lay for a few moments luxuriating in the memory of their lovemaking. Thinking about it alone made her pulses race afresh. Five days. That was all the time they had known one another. It scarcely seemed possible.

She had known Francisco little longer than that before going to bed with him, came the sudden and sobering reflection. She had believed herself in love with him too—or had that simply been a justification for allowing herself to give way to him in the first place? But there was surely no comparison between the way she had felt then and the way she felt now? Rafael was far more deserving of love than his brother had ever been.

The opening of the door brought her back to the present with a start. She rolled over just in time to receive the impact of two small but sturdy bodies as the twins took flying leaps on to the bed.

'Time to get up!' they chanted in unison.

It was apparent from the bright eyes and mischievous grins that yesterday's unfortunate episode was forgotten. Lauren gave a pretend groan and tried to burrow back under the cover. 'It's not even seven o'clock,' she protested.

'It's light already,' declared Nicolás, as if that were reason enough for everyone to be up and about. He pulled the sheet away, gazing with childish interest at her bare breasts. 'Why aren't you wearing any clothes?'

'I was too hot,' Lauren fabricated hastily, only just resisting the impulse to pull the sheet about her again. She had always taught the two of them to regard nudity as perfectly natural, with the female body no great secret; they would think it very strange indeed if she suddenly went all coy on them. 'How about going and playing with your trains while I get dressed?'

'OK,' said César obligingly. 'Come on, Nico.'

Her nudity was reflected in the long dressing mirror when she slid out from the bed. She took a moment to study the image, trying to see herself the way Rafael saw her. Men had such different priorities. Her own personal ideal was verging on the boyish, like catwalk models; they looked superb in whatever they wore.

For the wedding she would choose a classic style that would lend her poise and confidence, she thought dreamily. Deep cream, perhaps, with matching accessories and a picture hat trimmed in apricot. Rafael could wear a cream suit to tone; it wouldn't look out of place here.

She caught herself up at that point, smiling at her flight of fancy. Rafael would wear exactly what *he* chose to wear, toning or not. Clothes did not make the man.

Eager as she was to see him again, she knew a sense of let-down when he failed to put in an appearance at breakfast. Gabriel was missing too. He finally arrived just as she was about to depart after seeing the twins off with Elena.

Rafael had gone to Seville, he informed her. Something to do with their marriage, he thought, which made her feel a little better, although she would have liked the opportunity to go with him.

'He was also, I believe, intending to begin proceedings for the legal adoption of the twins,' Gabriel added.

'But they already have the name,' she said. 'What else is necessary?'

He shrugged. 'A matter of full control over their future, perhaps.'

Including their schooling, Lauren conjectured. She had forgotten until now about that particular issue. Still, there was plenty of time to sort things out. The adoption could hardly be finalised without her agreement.

'I'm going over to have coffee with Alicia this morning,' she said, by way of changing the subject. 'I take it that's all right with you?'

'Why should it not be?' Gabriel sounded totally indifferent.

'Just a thought. I'll need a car, of course.'

'Help yourself,' he invited. 'Carlos will supply you with the keys to either of those available.'

'You don't plan on going out yourself?' she ventured.

The shrug came again. 'Perhaps.'

'Oh, for heaven's sake, stop feeling sorry for yourself!' Lauren burst out exasperatedly. 'You didn't *have* to agree to this marriage.'

Even that failed to rouse him to any degree. 'What other choice was there?' he asked flatly. 'You know what Rafael threatened!'

'Only threatened. That's a long way from carrying out.'

'You have a lot to learn still about my brother. He makes no idle threats. If I'd failed to recognise the betrothal, I would have been forced to leave Callahora. You think that fair and just?'

She didn't, but it was a bit late to start backing down now. 'You have an income of your own,' she pointed out. 'Large enough, from what I understand, to provide you with all the security you'll ever need.'

'You would naturally take Rafael's side.' He still sounded emotionless. He pushed away his chair and rose from the table. 'I have work to do.'

She could have handled that better, acknowledged Lauren ruefully as he went from the room. No amount of upbraiding was going to make him see Alicia in a different light. There had to be some other way.

Carlos was the gatekeeper and general handyman. He handed over the keys to a green Lancia with some reluctance, and watched her closely as she reversed the car out of its parking space in the courtyard. Lauren gave him a cheery wave before heading out through the gateway.

The Floreses' hacienda was reached via the Seville road. It looked even more imposing by daylight than it had last night. What Señor Flores did for a living, Lauren had no idea, but he was certainly no pauper.

Alicia welcomed her with more enthusiasm than she had expected.

'I hoped you would come, but I thought you might change your mind,' she said. '*Padre* has gone to Ronda, and *Madre* is visiting, so we are all alone.'

Apart from a variety of staff, thought Lauren drily. She was glad that the older generation was absent. Their presence would have been a bit too restrictive.

Coffee was served outside on a paved patio which afforded a superb view of the mountain scenery. The temperature was somewhere in the low seventies and free of humidity, the sunlight sparkling. Better by far than the coastal climate, although Lauren supposed that the winters up here would level the odds a little.

Alicia seemed more animated this morning, causing Lauren to wonder if she found her parents' absence something of a relief too. Given a little help, she could probably look quite pretty, she thought, appraising her feature by feature. If she would only loosen her hair it would make such a difference. The coil at the nape of her neck was so thick that it must be waist-length at least. It was a shame to hide it away.

'You have such beautiful hair, Lauren,' Alicia remarked suddenly, almost as if picking up vibes. 'The colour is like evening sunlight!'

'That's the nicest compliment anyone ever paid me,' Lauren smiled. 'You have a wonderful turn of phrase.'

'I sometimes write poetry,' the other admitted diffidently. 'Only for my own entertainment, of course.'

'Do you ever find life boring?' asked Lauren on a casual note, and saw a smile touch the girl's mouth.

'Life is what one makes of it.'

'Like marriage,' Lauren agreed. 'You love Gabriel very much, don't you?'

The smile this time was wistful. 'More, I think, than he will ever feel for me. He is so handsome. He could have any wife he chose. When we were children we were good friends, but now he is a man it is different. He no longer sees me with the same eyes.'

The opening was there, Lauren judged, but she would need to proceed very carefully.

'Unfortunately, men tend to be that way,' she said. 'They judge by the packaging rather than the content. Short of changing their attitude, which isn't likely, our only recourse is to go along with it by making the best of what we have.'

Alicia eyed her with unexpected shrewdness. 'You are suggesting that I do not do this myself, perhaps?'

Total honesty, Lauren decided, was the only policy. She smiled and lifted her shoulders. 'Your hairstyle doesn't exactly flatter you. Why do you wear it like that?'

'Because it is neat and tidy,' came the answer.

'It must be very long,' Lauren commented. 'And it shines like silk!' She added softly, 'Why don't you let me show you how good it would look left loose? Most men love long hair!'

Alicia looked doubtful. 'I used to wear it so when I was a child, but not since I became a woman.'

Lauren laughed. 'I'm a good four years older than you, and I wear *my* hair down. Just try it. You can always put it up again if you feel too uncomfortable.'

The doubt gave way suddenly, lighting a spark of interest in the dark eyes. 'You do not mind doing this for me?'

'If I did, I wouldn't be here,' Lauren assured her.

They retired to Alicia's bedroom for the event. Like the rest of the hacienda, it was beautifully appointed. Sitting down at the dressing fitment, Alicia allowed Lauren to remove the lace snood and unpin the heavy coil of hair. Freed from its confinement, it fell just short of her waistline, its thickness springing into natural waves about her face.

'You see,' said Alicia despairingly. 'It is so disorderly!'

Gazing at her through the mirror, Lauren could hardly believe the transformation. She had often smiled at scenes in films and books where the hero released the heroine's hair to disclose a raving beauty, and dismissed the whole thing as romanticism, but it wasn't completely so. Framed within the tumbling cascade of glossy black hair, Alicia's face seemed to have altered shape, her features to havc acquired a new definition. Pretty, no, but *very* much morc attractive!

'It isn't unruly, it's lovely!' Her pleasure was uncontained. 'And so are you. Gabriel will have the surprise of his life when he sees you like this!'

Expression still uncertain as she looked at herself, Alicia said slowly, 'You really think it an improvement?'

More like a miracle, Lauren wanted to tell her, but that would have been going a bit over the top. 'I wouldn't lie to you,' she said instead. 'Promise me you'll give yourself a chance to get used to it?'

The girl was silent for a moment, viewing her reflection with furrowed brow. 'I must wait and see what *Madre* has to say,' she said at length.

Lauren bit back the instinctive comment. Diplomacy was the keyword. 'I'd think it rather more important to please Gabriel,' she returned mildly. 'But you must do as you see best, of course.'

'Yes.' Alicia gave her a sudden warm smile. 'I am very grateful for your interest in me, Lauren. Will you stay and eat luncheon?'

Rafael was unlikely to return from Seville until late in the day, she thought, and the twins were well taken care of. She smiled back, and nodded. 'I'd love to.'

Her suspicion that Alicia might want her here as much for support when Señora Flores returned as the pleasure of her company was confirmed when the latter did put in an appearance. Somewhat surprisingly, after the first startled comment, the newcomer seemed to accept her daughter's changed appearance with good grace. The lack of censure in itself increased Alicia's confidence. By the time her father returned she was able to face him with a sparkle in her eye and a look of expectancy rather than misgiving.

He didn't disappoint her, much to Lauren's relief, although his approval too was restrained. Politeness might be preventing them both from making their true feelings known in front of her, of course, in which case, she could only hope that Alicia wouldn't be deterred by any adverse comment when she had left. Gabriel couldn't fail to appreciate the change himself, even though it did only cover the packaging. As to the rest, well, that was up to him. All that was needed was encouragement.

Driving away later, she decided on impulse to take a detour through Ronda rather than use the Carretera de Circunvalación. She might even take the opportunity to browse through the shopping streets just to see what there was.

Despite the hour, the town was busy. Lauren found a place to park near the Alameda, and enjoyed a stroll through the gardens until she came out at the very edge of the gorge. The iron railings were protection enough for most against the sheer drop, she supposed, but they didn't make her feel any safer. She beat a hasty retreat to the street.

It was only then that she spotted the white coupé further down the row of parked vehicles. It looked familiar enough to draw her closer to where she could see the registration. Rafael's car, definitely. He must have called here on his way home from Seville.

They might even bump into one another, she thought, eager to see him again. He had to be somewhere not too far away.

It wasn't, however, to be, although she kept her eyes peeled for him. She walked the length of the Calle de la Bola and back again, enjoying the sights and sounds and glad that she wasn't a tourist here only for the day. She would need to go back to England at least once, of course, in order to sort everything out. The house would have to put on the market, and something done about the furniture et cetera. Apart from clothing and few personal items, there was nothing she really wanted to keep. She was leaving that part of her life behind.

The coupé was gone when she got back. Obviously Rafael hadn't spotted the Lancia, or he would surely have waited. On the other hand, she realised, he was still under the impression that she couldn't drive, so even if he had seen it he would have assumed that Gabriel had left it there.

She felt a bit guilty about the deception, but things had been different then. And she had never actually *said* she couldn't drive, had she?

Rafael was speaking with Carlos in the courtyard when she arrived back at Callahora. He waited until she had parked the car and got out before moving to meet her. He looked far from delighted to see her, she thought.

'Do you hold a licence?' he asked without preamble.

'Yes, I do,' she confirmed. 'The superintendent at the home taught me to drive as soon as I was old enough because he thought it might be an advantage when I left.'

'Then why,' he asked, 'did you lead me to believe you incapable?'

She shrugged uncomfortably. 'I thought it might make it easier to... borrow a car, if I had to.'

'For what purpose?'

'You know for what purpose,' she said. 'You'd just told me about cancelling our return tickets.'

'And you thought to drive back to England instead?'

Lauren had to smile. 'Well, obviously not all the way—unless you'd happened to have an amphibian stowed away somewhere.' She added, 'I'd have asked you if I could take a car if you'd been here to ask. I'd promised to go and see Alicia.'

The lean features had relaxed a little. 'It wasn't the car that concerned me so much as the belief that you were driving without proper authority and experience.'

'You really think me capable of doing something so stupid?' Lauren demanded with asperity, and saw a faint smile tug at the corners of his mouth.

'I would have used the word reckless, but yes, I think it possible. However, as you *are* qualified, after all, the Lancia is yours, if you would like it. All I ask is that you leave word of your whereabouts.'

'Gabriel knew where I'd gone,' she said, momentarily sidetracked.

'I have yet to see Gabriel,' came the dry reply, 'having only just returned myself. It was Carlos who told me of your departure this morning.' He paused. 'You were with Alicia all this time?'

'I had lunch there, then I went into Ronda. I saw your car parked just a short distance from mine, but you were gone when I got back.'

Some unreadable expression flickered across his face. 'Why did you go to Ronda?'

'Just to look at the shops.'

'I see no purchases.'

'I didn't see anything I wanted to buy.' She added lightly, 'Where were you?'

'I had business to conduct,' he said. 'I failed to notice the Lancia when I left.'

'I can only have been minutes behind you.' Lauren paused. 'You really mean it about the car?'

He searched her face for a moment, eyes intent, then he inclined his head. 'I try always to say what I mean. The car is yours. Just be sure you use it wisely.'

Accompanying him indoors, Lauren decided she must have imagined some underlying meaning in the caution.

What else could he have meant but to be careful on the roads? With transport available, and no limitations given, she could be as independent as she cared to be. In Isabella and Alicia she already had friends here, and hopefully more to come.

And, above all, there was Rafael himself. Lover now, husband to be. Imperfect though that relationship might seem at present, there was hope there too.

Judging from their enthusiastic account of various activities, the twins had had an excellent day too, although Lauren had the feeling that Elena was keeping something back when she assured her that they had behaved themselves well. César had badly scraped knees, injuries supposedly sustained when he slipped while playing football. It seemed unlikely to Lauren that grass would have caused such an injury, but she accepted the story at face value.

It was only later, when she was changing for dinner, that she remembered she still had to discuss the subject of the boys' education with Rafael. If what Gabriel had said was true, then arrangements for the private tutor might already have been made, but that didn't mean she had to agree to it. Her emotional involvement with the man she was to marry was no surrender of rights. That was something he still had to comprehend. When it came to schooling, the twins would surely be better off working alongside other children rather than alone.

She had forgotten also that they were to entertain Dr Manvers and his wife to dinner this evening. Finding the two of them already seated with Rafael in the *salón* when she got down was a surprise she made every effort to conceal.

There were just the four of them. Gabriel, it appeared, was out. Lauren hoped he would have gone to see Alicia, but somehow doubted it. The wedding date had been set, his fate sealed; he was probably drowning his sorrows in some bar, or dancing them away in a disco.

It was a pleasant evening. Having stayed at Callahora several times in the past, the American couple had already established an unceremonious relationship with their host, and were easy to be with. Lauren found the doctor's dry humour an entertainment in itself. Although coming close to retirement from his profession, he was still young at heart, his wife likewise.

'I'm glad to see your young rascal so fully recovered from his fever, by the way,' he said when they were leaving. 'Although I'd keep a sharp eye on his climbing activities. That was a nasty fall he took this afternoon. If the girl hadn't caught him, it could have been a lot worse.'

'Where exactly did you see him climbing?' asked Rafael.

'On the perimeter wall. I think he'd gone up the steps near the entrance, and tried to get down again from the walkway further along.' He smiled and shook his head. 'Boys will be boys! My own two were always up to some daredevil scheme.'

'You're telling tales out of school,' said his wife on a light note. 'There was no real harm done.'

'Coming from somebody who spent years of her life worrying about what our kids were up to, that's rich!' he scoffed good-humouredly. 'Tale or not, it needed telling.'

'And we're grateful that you did,' Rafael assured him before Lauren could speak. 'He will certainly not be climbing up there again.'

'Did you already know about this?' he demanded after the other couple had departed.

'I knew he'd grazed his knees,' Lauren admitted. 'And I'll certainly be giving him a ticking-off in the morning for not telling me the truth.'

'I think,' Rafael said grimly, 'that I had best deal with the matter. Both of them need to be taught a sharp lesson.'

'Why both?' she asked. 'So you can be sure of punishing the right one?' She met his gaze squarely. 'I'll handle it myself.'

'The same way you handled their last escapade?' His tone was clipped. 'Would you prefer to have one, or even both of them killed or maimed for life for want of a little applied discipline now?'

There was something in what he was saying, Lauren knew, but she wasn't about to let it go at that. 'Has it occurred to you,' she enquired icily, 'that your precious nursemaid was lacking in supervision in the first place?'

'Certainly it occurred to me,' he said. 'She will be dismissed.'

Lauren gazed at him in sudden dismay, sorry now for bringing the girl into it. 'That isn't fair,' she protested. 'Not for one mistake. If anyone is to blame, it's me for letting you arrange things in the first place. I should have been with them myself.'

'That,' he said, 'is an issue to be discussed another time. Right or wrong, *I* employed the girl, and *I* will make whatever decision I think necessary. As to César...' he eyed her contemplatively for a moment, then gave a brusque nod '...I'll speak with him in the morning.'

'Speak?' Lauren queried.

'Just that.' He lifted a sardonic brow at her hesitation. 'You will just have to trust my word.'

'All right,' she said. 'I'll trust you. But only if you promise to give Elena another chance.'

'I was under the impression that you wished to take full care of the boys yourself from now on? Or did I mistake your meaning?'

Lauren bit her lip. 'I said it off the top of my head. They think the world of Elena. I don't want to smother them with mother-love.'

'A commendable attitude,' Rafael approved, 'but it fails to alter the fact that the girl was neglectful in her duties.'

'I'm sure she'll keep a closer watch on the pair of them in future.'

He said firmly, 'The decision is mine.'

Anger flared in her. 'In this instance, perhaps, but not in everything! I may as well tell you now that I've no intention of accepting private tutorship, no matter what you've arranged! They need to be with other children.'

'Even at the cost of their advancement?' Rafael was angry himself; that was evident from the glitter in his eyes. 'The school best qualified to teach gifted children is many miles away, and they would need to board. Would you prefer that?'

Lauren made a helpless little gesture. 'There has to be some kind of compromise.'

'A condition in which you place much faith,' he said drily, 'but not, unfortunately, always possible to achieve. I agree that they have need of other children as playmates, which can easily be arranged. It would also help them with their Spanish. Their educational needs are a different matter. These early years, when they are at their most receptive, are the most important of their lives. Would you deny them their full potential?'

What he said made sense, Lauren was forced to admit. The twins were special, and had to be treated as such.

Sending them away to school was totally out of the question, of course, which left little choice.

'Is it just your sons' welfare that concerns you so much,' asked Rafael shrewdly, studying her, 'or my assumption of authority?'

She couldn't bring herself to look at him directly, too well aware that he'd hit the nail on the head. Loving him as a man didn't preclude resentment of his masculine assertion.

'I think,' he said after a moment, 'that we should put the matter aside for now and concentrate instead on more immediate affairs. As I've told you before, it isn't your subjugation I look for.'

'Are you sure?' Her voice was low. 'Because you'll never have it!'

His smile was slow. 'But I have this...'

Lauren made no attempt to evade him as he reached for her. She badly needed the reaffirmation of his desire for her. There would come a time when it wasn't enough for him, but that time hadn't yet come—not when he could kiss her with such hunger. It was even possible that he found her opposition a stimulant in itself, she thought, as he slid both hands down her back to bring her hips into closer proximity with his. He was already fully and thrillingly aroused.

Wakening still wrapped in his arms in the dim, pre-dawn light, she knew a moment or two of sheer contentment before the doubts took over again. No matter how wonderful this part of their relationship was, it still left a whole lot wanting. Rafael might not even be capable of love the way she saw it, but was *she* capable of settling for less?

'I think I had better be going before the boys decide to pay you a visit,' he murmured, giving her a shock because she had thought him still asleep. He came up on an elbow to place a light kiss on her forehead, his jawline rough on her cheek. 'You continue to surprise me, *mi amada*,' he added softly. 'Such fire in an Englishwoman!'

'Only when fed,' she whispered, and saw his mouth briefly widen.

'Then I must make sure to conserve my energies.'

Lauren found it difficult to stop herself from putting out a restraining hand as he slid from the bed. He was right; the door was unlocked and the twins could waken any time. Having already accepted Rafael as a substitute husband and father, they might not think there was anything untoward in his being here, but she would rather they remained in ignorance until after the wedding—if only to be sure they didn't go telling anyone they'd seen Uncle Rafael in Mummy's bed.

Hypocrite! she thought wryly.

Unable to sleep again, she got up at six-thirty, pulling on a cotton wrap before going through to check on the twins. The sight of two empty beds didn't disturb her too much at first. Not until she found the bathroom vacant too did she start to worry. She didn't even know how long they'd been gone, she realised, although the mattresses still held a faint body warmth, so it couldn't be *that* long.

If Rafael got to know they'd gone missing again, they'd be in real trouble. And rightfully so; this time she had to agree. There were too many dangers here for the two of them to wander about the place on their own. She could only hope that they hadn't gone up to the roof again.

She went up the tower steps as quietly as she could. Rafael's bedroom door was ajar, the bathroom door closed. She took the narrower flight at a fair speed. Going up wasn't so much of a problem; it was coming down again that caused the vertigo.

It was a vast relief to find the circular roof empty, but that only lasted as long as it took her to realise that they could already have fallen over the parapet if they'd been playing the same games. Her heart in her mouth, she shuffled across the intervening space to the nearest embrasure on hands and knees, grasping the parapet at its lowest point and taking a deep breath before wriggling the upper half of her body out over the thickness of wall to look down at the ground far below.

The light was good enough by now to see that no small broken bodies lay there. At least, not on this side. She would need to repeat the performance a couple of times more to be perfectly sure, she told herself desperately.

Her head was swimming; she felt as if something were drawing her down. She could find neither strength nor will to draw herself back to safety, but just lay there with the blood drumming louder and louder into her ears.

The hands seizing her about the waist were steel-like in their grip. Rafael yanked her upright, spinning her round to face him with a force almost as dizzying as the vertigo itself. His whole face was tensed, his eyes like coals.

'What the devil do you think you're doing?' he demanded.

Face as white as a sheet, limbs refusing to support her any longer, she swayed against him. 'I was afraid they might have fallen over,' she got out. 'I had to see!'

His expression altered. 'They came up here again?'

'I don't know. They weren't in their room. This was the first place I thought of.' She was babbling, she knew, but she couldn't stop. 'They might still be down there. I only looked this side.'

He half carried her across to the central block, standing her with her back against solid stone. 'Stay there,' he ordered superfluously.

Throat dry, Lauren watched him go to each embrasure in turn and look over, closing her eyes in glad relief when he turned away from the last with a shake of his head.

'So now we go and find them,' he said grimly, coming back to her. 'And this time they will suffer the consequences of their disobedience.'

Lauren was too wrought up for dispute. Their safety still wasn't certain. She followed Rafael down the steps as she had done twice before, struggling to conquer the lingering effects.

She had hoped that the twins would have returned to their bedroom by the time they reached it, but they hadn't. Nor was there any sign that they'd been there since her last visit. Rafael led the way downstairs in silence, face expressionless.

They weren't in the *salón*, or dining-room, nor had the kitchen staff seen them. If they'd taken it into their heads to explore the guest regions, they could be anywhere, thought Lauren despairingly. The dungeons, for instance.

It was Rafael who opened the library door. Seated on the floor in their pyjamas, the two of them were surrounded by books taken from the shelves. That they knew they were doing wrong was evidenced by the guilt written large in each face.

'We're only looking,' claimed César. 'We haven't damaged them.'

Lauren resisted the urge to go and gather them up in sheer relief. This was Rafael's domain; it had to be his place to decide the penalty, much as she wanted to protest. The lack of anger in his voice when he spoke surprised her.

'You should not have left your room at all without permission, should you?'

'No,' agreed Nicolás, looking downcast. 'But——'

'No buts,' Rafael said firmly. 'You put every one of those back in place, then you go to your room until breakfast. And in future you ask permission before you take any book from the shelves. Some of them are very old and fragile.' He put out a hand as Lauren made an instinctive movement. 'No. They took them out, they must put them back.'

She subsided without protest. It was fair enough, especially after he had held back on the threatened chastisement. To 'old and fragile' he could have added 'valuable', but he hadn't. He was trusting the two of them to take care.

Which they did. Even at this age, they had an inherent reverence for books of any kind, Lauren reflected, watching them with a certain pride. They could have understood comparatively little of the actual writing in the ones they had been looking at, but the interest alone was enough to be going on with. Books were the key to a whole new world; they already understood that.

Barefooted, they scampered back up to their room when released, leaving mother and uncle to follow on at their own pace.

'Thanks for not being too angry with them,' Lauren said gratefully. 'You had every reason to be.'

Rafael smiled and shrugged. 'Had they been anywhere else, I would have spanked them both for causing you distress, but it would have been difficult to separate one transgression from the other. Their interest in reading matter must be encouraged, not repressed.' He added firmly, 'I shall still be having words with them about yesterday's escapade, however.'

They had reached the landing. Lauren did her best to keep her tone impartial as she said, 'And Elena?'

There was a brief pause, then he nodded his head in resigned recognition of her unspoken plea. 'She may stay.'

'Thanks,' Lauren said again.

A hint of amusement sprang in his eyes. 'You're welcome.'

She had to laugh herself. 'Americanisms just don't suit you!'

'You find Spanish responses more to your taste?'

Any day of the week, she thought. On impulse, she went up on tiptoe to press her lips to a jaw freshly shaven, only now becoming conscious that he was fully dressed. 'That's for being who you are,' she said.

His expression was difficult to read, his tone equally so. 'Does that mean you accept me the way I am?'

Lauren kept her own tone light, lacking the courage to tell him the truth. 'I don't really have a great deal of choice, do I?'

'No more than I have myself.' He nodded brusquely and turned away, leaving her standing there feeling depressed again. Would there ever come a time when she could say the words she longed to say to him? she wondered.

CHAPTER TEN

THE twins were subdued after a private talk with their uncle, but had regained their normal high spirits by mid-morning. Elena, Lauren noted, was slower to recover from reproof. She looked thoroughly downcast.

'I am so sorry that I failed to tell you the truth,' she said at the first opportunity. 'It was wrong of me to hide it from you. The fault was wholly mine in not watching César more closely.'

'The fault was his in climbing up there at all,' Lauren replied firmly. 'He knows he shouldn't. Anyway, you saved him from a far worse injury.'

'It was fortunate that I was close enough to catch him.' The girl hesitated. 'Don Rafael said it is only because of your pleading that he allows me to stay. I am very grateful for your trust, *señora*.'

Trust Rafael to interpret her request that way, thought Lauren with wry humour. Not that it really mattered. The result was all she cared about. Elena was both good with the boys and intelligent in her own right. One only had to take her excellent grasp of the English language as evidence of her learning ability. It might even be possible for her to extend her own education when this private tutor arrived. Teaching two small boys was hardly going to tax the man.

That it would be a man, she didn't for a moment doubt. Rafael would consider a female tutor less than adequate.

He was missing at lunchtime. Neither did Gabriel profess to know this time where he'd gone.

'I do what I'm given to do,' he said. 'I don't question my brother's movements. It's possible that he went to Ronda.'

Lauren studied him for a moment, struck by something in his tone. 'What business does he have in Ronda?'

Gabriel shrugged. 'He was considering one of the hotels near the Alameda. He may still have an interest.'

That was probably where he would have been yesterday, she conjectured. He had said it was business. 'How big is it?' she asked.

'Not too large.' The pause seemed deliberated. 'Nina Ortega inherited it from a cousin with no family of his own, but she had no interest in keeping it—or so I understood. It would need a great deal of work to bring it up to Quiros standards, but that is Rafael's business, of course. I have no say in the matter.'

Lauren was listening with only half an ear. She felt as if the bottom had dropped right out of her world. Nina Ortega. It would have to be, wouldn't it? Not the kind of woman Rafael would ever have considered marrying, Isabella had declared with such certainty, but apparently the kind of woman—if that was where he had gone again today—fit to continue as his mistress. Small wonder that she'd looked with such bitter animosity on the one who *was* deemed fit to be his wife.

And what kind of man was it, Lauren asked herself, who would deliberately bring the two of them together the way he had? He had arranged it to show the woman her place. She had thought him ruthless to start with, but this went beyond that. Brutality would be nearer the mark!

Picking up the vibes, the twins were looking at her curiously. She made an effort to smile at them and start eating again. Gabriel made no further comment. There was no need. He knew she had grasped the point.

It was only after the twins had been excused that he made some attempt at reparation.

'It was wrong of me to suggest that Rafael might have gone to see Nina,' he said. 'He didn't tell me *where* he was going.'

'It doesn't matter,' she returned unemotionally, and saw his look of surprise.

'You have no objection to his... friendship with another woman?'

'Why should I?' she asked in the same flat tone. 'He's still free to do whatever he wants to do.'

'And after the two of you are married?'

Green eyes lifted to return his gaze without a flicker. 'There isn't going to be any marriage.'

'Don't say that,' he protested, looking suddenly alarmed. 'I may well be mistaken in thinking he is still seeing her!'

'I doubt it,' she said. 'He was with her yesterday.'

'You saw them together?'

Lauren hesitated. 'Not exactly. I saw his car parked near the Alameda. But where else would he have been?'

'But even if he was looking again at the Marisa you have no proof that Nina was with him. If he is there again now, you still have no proof of his intention.'

Which was true enough, Lauren conceded. She only had the suspicion planted so slyly by Gabriel himself.

'So I'll go and see for myself,' she declared decisively, getting up from the table. 'The Marisa, you said?'

'Yes.' Her brother-in-law looked anything but happy. 'Is it wise, do you think, to go there?'

It was Lauren's turn to shrug. 'Probably not. I may still be left guessing if I don't find them together, but I'll deal with that if and when.'

She went upstairs to get a purse and change her shoes for a pair with lower heels. The sun had retreated behind a blanket of cloud when she got outside, causing a sharp drop in temperature. She could have done with a jacket of some kind over the crisp cotton shirt she was wearing, but she would be in the car for the most part, she reasoned, reluctant to delay any further. The temperature would be her least concern if suspicion turned out to be fact.

The cloud grew steadily thicker as she drove towards the town. By the time she reached the plaza where she had parked the previous day, it was looking more and more like rain coming.

Finding the Marisa was no great problem, because it was right there on the corner—a three-storeyed building with balconied windows fronting on to the plaza. Far from a Quiros-type property at present, Lauren judged, though that wasn't to say it could never be.

There was no sign of the white coupé today, but that didn't necessarily mean Rafael wasn't here. Knowing she had spotted it yesterday, he might have decided to park it well away from the Marisa this time, just in case.

The main doors opened into a shabby reception area. There was no one on duty at the scarred desk set across the rear wall, and no sign of movement from what Lauren took to be the office, although the door was open. Only when she rang the wooden-handled bell did a man in the inevitable black trousers and white shirt of the serving class emerge reluctantly from the inner confines, not even attempting to smother a cavernous yawn.

Siesta, of course, Lauren realised. Up until that moment, she hadn't given much thought to what she was going to say. Faced with the newcomer's grouchy enquiry, she found herself floundering.

'Do you know Señor de Quiros?' she got out.

'*Sí*,' he said.

'Is he here now? In the hotel?'

'Now?' The man shook his head. 'No.'

The relief was fleeting. 'Was he here yesterday, then?'

He considered the words for a moment or two before his brow cleared. '*Ayer, sí!*'

So that, she thought hollowly, was that. Yet she had to be sure. 'Señorita Ortega?' she said. 'She was here too?'

'*Sí*.' He was beginning to lose what little interest he had managed to summon at all. 'You want room?'

Lauren shook her head. The two of them being here in the hotel at the same time was still no positive proof of their ongoing personal involvement, but why else would Rafael have turned the question of his whereabouts aside? With no shortage of bedrooms to choose from, what better place to conduct their affairs?

It was raining when she got outside again—and not gently either. She was soaked to the skin by the time she reached the car. There was nowhere else to go but Callahora, of course. The twins alone were reason enough for her return.

What she was going to do from here on in, she had no clear idea. Facing Rafael with duplicity was no solution when all he had to do was deny it. And, even if he admitted it, he wasn't going to allow her to take the twins away without a fight. Which left her right back where she had started—loving him and hating him at one and the same time. A thin line indeed.

It was still raining when she reached the castle. Hair hanging damply about her face, shirt still clinging to her, she drew solicitous comment from Carlos—at least, that was what she took it to be.

A warm shower and a change of clothing was her first priority, she decided. After that, she had to think long and hard and constructively. If marriage was out, what was the alternative?

She reached her room without seeing anyone. Judging by the sounds coming from the twins' room, they were playing some kind of word game with Elena, and in Spanish! The two of them would be bilingual by the time they were ready to start their schooling proper.

Could she even contemplate tearing them away from all the advantages they had here? Lauren asked herself disconsolately. They were happy, they were fulfilled, they were secure—all the things she had been too until Gabriel had opened up this new can of worms for her. They had to come first; that was certain. No matter what the cost.

Warmed through physically if no other way by the shower, she put on a pair of white trousers and a peach-coloured cotton sweater. She had shampooed her hair too, and towelled it dry. Still damp, it fell smooth and shining to her centre back. Her face looked pinched through the mirror, her eyes lacklustre. Hardly surprising, she supposed, in the circumstances.

The knock on the door jerked every nerve in her body. Not the twins, for sure; they would have come bursting in pell-mell. She went to open it, feeling her heart do a painful double flip as she looked at the man standing there.

'Carlos informs me that you were soaking wet when you came in,' he said, taking in her appearance. 'What possessed you to go out in the rain without protection?'

'I didn't know it was going to rain.' Lauren was surprised at the steadiness of her voice. 'I got caught out.'

'You went to Ronda again?' Rafael asked.

'That's right.' She could even smile, she found. 'I want to get to know the place.'

'You have plenty of time to do that.' He was smiling himself, eyes appraising her face. 'Few women could dispense with artificial aids and still look so delightful.'

And what did he tell Nina? Lauren asked herself, trying to ignore the undeniable pull at her heartstrings. He was practised in the art of pleasing women, practised in every angle of seduction.

'Thank you,' she said lightly, 'but I think I'll settle for a little help anyway—as I was about to do when you knocked. The twins are in their room with Elena, if you want to see them.'

His regard sharpened a fraction, as if in recognition of some subtle difference in her. He wanted to come in, Lauren knew, but she dared not allow him to. He was too capable of making her forget everything else.

'Yes,' he said, 'I want to see them. They invited me to play trains again, if you remember.'

She pretended not to notice the irony. 'I'm sure they'll be delighted.' Desperate for him to go, she added, 'I might come and play myself when I've finished getting ready. It's a fascinating pastime.'

'Like many others,' he agreed.

Lauren closed the door as he turned away, and drew in a shaky breath. Things obviously couldn't continue this way. Rafael was going to want to know what was wrong with her if she tried keeping him at a distance. She had surrendered herself to him too ardently only last night for him to believe that she had suddenly lost all desire for his attentions.

So what was left but the truth? He wouldn't take kindly to an ultimatum, but he must take note of it. She was prepared to stay here for the twins' sakes, but not to marry him unless he could convince her that he was finished with Nina once and for all. That would be the choice she offered him.

She left it as long she could before going through to the other room, only to find it empty. It had stopped raining quite some time ago, and the sun was out once more, so no doubt they were all outside somewhere.

Lauren knew a sudden longing for it to be just the three of them again, with only the basic financial problems to worry about. She would have managed. Others did. Wasn't it always said that what you never had you never missed?

She saw nothing of Rafael again until they met in the *salón* before dinner. He was a little reserved in his greeting, but as solicitous as ever in seeing her comfortably seated and supplying her with a drink.

'Is Gabriel out tonight?' she asked, hoping against hope that the answer would be no. The dinner table was no place for what she had in mind. She needed more time to gather herself.

'I have no idea,' he returned. 'If he planned to be, he will, I hope, have informed Juanita. She has enough to do without preparing meals for those not here to eat them.'

Considering the amount of food served even for two, Lauren doubted if it would make much difference. She looked down at the glass in her hand, rolling the slender stem between nerveless fingers. Less than a week ago she had sat here drinking sherry with a total stranger. From there to this was a leap difficult to credit.

Rafael hadn't taken a seat but was standing by the great fireplace. She could see him from the corner of her eye, lean and lithe in the close-fitting black trousers and cream silk shirt. The latter was opened at the throat, revealing the St Christopher medal he wore. Given him many years ago by his mother, he had told her, and never removed since. The chain itself was soldered together.

'I think you had better say whatever it is you have on your mind,' he stated expressionlessly. 'I have no intention of sitting through dinner in such an atmosphere.'

'I wasn't aware there was an atmosphere,' she said, playing for time to marshal her suddenly scattered thoughts. She had reckoned on choosing her own moment, not have it thrust on her so abruptly.

'Don't take me for a fool. It was apparent this afternoon that something was troubling you.' His tone was sharper now. 'So tell me!'

No time, and no choice, Lauren thought ruefully. She steeled herself to look at him directly. 'I went to the Marisa today.'

His only visible reaction was a lifted brow. 'Why?'

'To find out if you were there.'

'And what discovery did you make?'

'That you were there yesterday—along with Nina Ortega!'

'From which you assumed... what?'

'You know what!' She had come to the very edge of her seat, body tensed. 'If there was nothing to hide, why did you lie to me about where you'd been?'

'I have no recollection of lying to you,' he said. 'I told you I was in Ronda on business.'

'But not what kind!'

He deposited his glass on the stone mantel without taking his gaze from her face. 'And what kind would *you* say it was?'

'The only kind you know, where a woman is concerned! The difference being that, while *she* might be willing to share your favours, *I'm* not!'

The skin about his mouth whitened as his teeth came together. 'So you offer me a choice?'

It was all going wrong, thought Lauren distraughtly. She hadn't meant to come right out with the accusation that way. Only it was too late now to retract. It had been said, and she had to stand by it. It was true, anyway. He would have denied it otherwise.

'That's right,' she responded with determination. 'A choice. Me, or her.'

'And should I choose Nina, what then?'

The lack of hesitation shook her. He wasn't even bothering to put up a fight. But then, why should he? Whatever he had had from her, Nina could almost certainly better. Pride came to her rescue, lending her control of both voice and emotions.

'I shan't attempt to take the twins away, if that's what you're thinking. You can give them a lot more than I can on my own.'

It was impossible to tell what he *was* thinking. His whole face looked set in granite. 'You mean you would be willing to leave them here?'

'No!' She was panic-stricken at the very suggestion. 'I most certainly didn't mean that! I'd be staying with them, naturally.'

'Let me be sure I have the meaning clear, then,' he said. 'If I refuse to give you my word that I have no involvement with Nina Ortega, our marriage will be cancelled, but you will still expect to make your home here. Is that correct?'

Lauren gazed at him defensively. 'I couldn't leave without Nicolás and César.'

'And I would be expected to treat you as a sister?' Rafael went on as if she hadn't spoken. 'You really think that possible after all we've been to each other?'

'It would have to be,' she said. She was hurting all over now. 'After all, you'd still have Nina to console you.'

He took a step towards her, eyes suddenly blazing, then pulled up abruptly as Gabriel came through the door. The atmosphere in the room was electric; the newcomer was immediately aware of it, looking from one to the other in speculation.

'I think I chose a bad moment,' he said. 'Shall I leave you?'

His brother was the first to respond; Lauren couldn't say a word. 'No need. It's time we went in to dinner.' His glance came back to her, devoid once more of expression. 'Are you ready?'

Lauren walked through ahead of them both, back rigid. Taking her place at table, she avoided looking at Gabriel seated opposite. If he had kept his mouth shut at lunchtime none of this would have happened.

But she would have found out some time, came the small voice of reason, and perhaps too late. She should be grateful to Gabriel for opening her eyes to his brother's true character—or this one facet of it, at least. He was genuine enough where the twins' welfare was concerned, she was sure. They were of the same blood.

Without seeming to make any particular effort, Rafael conducted a normal conversation throughout the meal. It being family only, the courses were limited to four instead of the innumerable dishes of the more formal affair, but Lauren had difficulty in eating anything at all. Her throat felt raw, as if she were coming down with a cold.

Coffee was served back in the *salón*, with Lauren presiding over the heavy silver pot. When, she wondered, handing Rafael his cup, would he see fit to renew the interrupted hostilities? He had been on the verge of committing some physical abuse, she believed; he had certainly looked angry enough. She couldn't bring herself to look at him directly.

'I went to pay a duty call on Alicia earlier,' said Gabriel as he took his cup from her.

She managed a smile, a touch of whimsy. 'How did you find her?'

'Looking very... different.' He was smiling too, albeit faintly. 'Your doing, I believe?'

'Just a suggestion.' She paused, aware that Rafael was listening. 'So what did you think?'

'That she's more attractive than I believed,' he admitted. 'And perhaps not quite so docile either. She accused me of shaming her, when only three days ago she was so grateful that we were to be married at all. Are you responsible for that too?'

'All I said was that you admired women with minds of their own,' Lauren declared. 'Obviously she has one.'

'She never showed sign of it before this.'

'Perhaps because she'd been brainwashed into believing her only role in life was to venerate the male of the species.'

The sudden bite in her voice drew a sharpened glance but no comment. It was left to Rafael to say sardonically, 'You might find she has something to teach you too.'

Lauren made herself look at him, hating him for the power he had to disturb her. 'I dare say she has. I'd be the last to claim flawlessness.'

'Speaking of marriage,' put in Gabriel with some diffidence, 'what date did you set for your own?'

There was no hesitation in the reply. 'Four weeks from today.' He held Lauren's gaze challengingly. 'Long enough in the circumstances.'

He was relying on her being reluctant to reissue her ultimatum in front of Gabriel, she conjectured. Which she was. Only he needn't think she was going to retract it either. Arrangements could always be unmade.

Sensing the conflict, Gabriel let the subject drop and made an effort instead to steer conversation into more general channels. Lauren kept an eye on the time, intending to claim tiredness as an excuse for an early retirement. Early by Spanish standards, at any rate. They kept unholy hours.

Rafael beat her to it. 'You will excuse me if I leave you,' he said formally. 'I have matters still to take care of.'

With one of them sitting right here, Lauren conjectured. He intended to be waiting for her when she went up to her room, she was certain. And with what in mind?

'I'm not in the least bit tired yet,' she lied. 'Gabriel will keep me company—won't you?'

'Of course,' he agreed.

The older man made no comment, simply nodded and went from the room. Lauren turned to Gabriel with an over-bright smile.

'Do you like the new Alicia, or would you rather have the old model back?'

'The differences are not so great,' he said. 'But they are encouraging. It will be interesting to discover what other surprises she may have in store for me.' He paused, expression pensive as he studied her face. 'Tell me, does the hostility between you and Rafael have to do with what I suggested to you at lunch?'

Her first instinct was to deny it. But what was the use? she asked herself wryly. He might as well have the truth.

'You knew I was going to the Marisa this afternoon,' she said.

'I know you threatened to go. I hoped you might change your mind.'

'Well, I didn't.'

Gabriel looked rueful. 'You found him with Nina?'

'Not exactly. He wasn't there today. The desk clerk told me they were both there yesterday, though.'

Dark brows drew together. 'Just that?'

'Isn't it enough?' she defended. 'Rafael doesn't intend buying that place. It's just an excuse to be with her!'

'They could be that without going to such lengths, I think,' Gabriel returned. He paused, obviously ill-at-ease. 'What I said to you earlier was intended to cause trouble between you. I've always been jealous of Rafael—and most especially since you came to Callahora. I knew from the way he looked at you the very first time that he intended to have you for himself, and I wanted to stop him. Only he was the one *you* wanted, not me.'

'I'm sorry.' Lauren hardly knew what else to say. 'I didn't . . . realise.'

He smiled and shrugged. 'I think you did. You must be accustomed to being desired.'

'Not essentially,' she denied, with memories of those last two years with Francisco. 'And if that's the only sentiment I inspire in a man I'll manage without one at all!'

'You believe Rafael feels nothing more for you?'

'I know it,' she said. 'He only offered marriage at all because of the twins.'

Gabriel looked thoughtful. 'I can't imagine him going so far for that reason only.'

'You said yourself that he could be ruthless,' she reminded him.

'Where there was no other alternative, yes. But he could have persuaded you to stay without marrying you.'

'Except that I wasn't prepared——' She broke off, biting her lip as she saw sudden comprehension dawn in his eyes.

'You were not prepared to give yourself to him without marriage; is that what you mean?'

'It wasn't like that,' Lauren protested. 'It never even occurred to me until he brought it up.'

'Which he would only have done if he truly wanted it.' Gabriel leaned towards her, emphasising his words. 'Even if Rafael was with Nina yesterday it need not mean that they were intimate together. Did you ask him outright?'

No, she hadn't, Lauren acknowledged, recalling those fraught few moments. All she had done was accuse him of lying. True, he had made no attempt to refute the implication, but then she hadn't given him much of an opportunity, had she, issuing that ultimatum the way she did? Running off at the mouth, it was called. Not exactly unknown for her.

If he was indeed waiting for her in her room, as she anticipated, then that would be the time to lay the whole thing on the line. His anger might have cooled enough to be reasonable about it all. The past wasn't her concern; it was the future she needed to be sure of. Just his word on it was all she asked.

'I think I'd better sleep on it,' she said.

'I think that may be a good idea,' Gabriel agreed. 'Problems always seem smaller in the morning.'

Not unless they've been resolved overnight, she thought, but she let the remark pass. He probably didn't believe it either.

She left him finishing off his brandy, mounting the spiral stairs with fast-beating heart. Her room door was closed. She hesitated outside it for a brief moment before turning away to go and check on the twins.

Fast asleep, they had both of them kicked off the thin duvets. She covered them up again, feeling the familiar flooding mother-love as she kissed each small face. They belonged here, even if she didn't. She couldn't leave them, and she couldn't take them away. Whatever else happened, this was home from now on—for them all.

Outside her own door again, she steadied herself before turning the ornate iron knob. The room was in darkness, but it was obviously empty; she would, she knew, have sensed Rafael's presence immediately. The emotions flooding her now were confused. She wasn't sure whether it was disappointment or relief that took precedence.

This problem wasn't going to seem any better in the morning, she told herself resolutely. It had to be settled tonight. If Rafael wouldn't come to her, then she had to go to him.

It wasn't an easy thing to do. Twice she almost turned round on the steps and came back. Rafael's bedroom door was closed too. She tapped on it, gently at first, and then again with increased vigour when there was no answer.

If anything, the lack of response served to harden her purpose. The door wasn't locked; it opened smoothly and silently to her touch. Rafael wasn't responding to the summons because he wasn't there, she found. Nor was he taking a shower, she judged from the lack of discarded clothing. Which left the library as the most likely place for him to be. Matters to take care of, he had said.

No turning back now, she decided. The library was as good a place as any in which to sort out their lives. She either emerged from there as Rafael's future wife, or merely as his sister-in-law. Either way, she would know where she stood.

She slipped on a step going down, and almost fell, but saved herself with the handrail. High heels were lethal on worn bare stone. Rafael had warned her about it that first day. Assertiveness for the sake of it rather than genuine concern for her welfare, she had thought at the time, so she hadn't taken much note. Pigheaded wasn't in it!

She didn't bother to knock on the library door, but went straight on in. Seated at the desk, Rafael looked up with drawn brows from the papers he was studying, expression undergoing an abrupt alteration when he saw who the intruder was. Not angry, Lauren thought, but not welcoming either.

'If you are here with the intention of repeating your ultimatum, I'd advise you to think again,' he said hardily. 'I'm in no tolerant frame of mind.'

Lauren found her voice steadier than she had anticipated. 'I'm here just to ask you one straight question,' she said. '*Do* you still have any involvement with Nina Ortega?'

For a long moment she thought he wasn't going to answer, then he said flatly, 'Yes.'

Her heart dropped like a stone. So there she had it. No punches pulled. She would almost rather have had him lie about it.

'But not of an intimate nature,' he added.

She gazed at him in silence, trying to come to grips with her warring emotions. 'Then what?' she got out.

'As I told you yesterday—a business affair. The Marisa is now part of the Quiros group.'

'But it's such a run-down place. Not a bit like the others.'

'It will be restored, naturally, although it will retain the same character and cater for a different class of clientele. Nina was threatening to sell it to developers. I could not allow that.'

Lauren said slowly, 'I'd have thought she would refuse to sell to you on principle alone.'

He gave a brief dry smile. 'The offer proved too alluring in the end.' He paused, studying her, eyes unrevealing. 'I would have told you all this earlier had you not drawn your own conclusions so swiftly. If you're not prepared to believe what I say, then I can do little about it.'

'I was blind with jealousy,' she admitted huskily. 'I couldn't bear to think of you with her. I can't bear to think of you with *any* other woman, if it comes to that. I know you don't believe in love, but it doesn't make any difference to the way I feel about you.'

'Not believe,' he repeated. 'Is that what you think?' He got to his feet, eyes no longer veiled as he came round the desk to take her in his arms, but fired by an emotion that caught her breath. 'You are more to me than life itself!' he declared fiercely. 'How can you not know what I feel for you when you possess my very soul?'

The kiss was almost savage in its intensity, but Lauren welcomed the bruising force, kissing him back with a fervency of her own. There was no doubt left in her heart now. He loved her! He really did love her! How could she ever have doubted it?

He swung her up and carried her over to a sofa, sitting down with her across his knees to kiss her again with the same passionate emotion.

'I can never have enough of you, *mi querida*,' he declared roughly. 'You fill my days with longing for you, my nights with pleasure greater than ever I imagined could exist!' His hand caressed her cheek with a touch so tender that it brought a lump to her throat. 'For some, love is slow to blossom, for others swift and fierce. I knew the moment I saw you that here was the woman I had waited for all my life. I regretted that my brother had found you first, but if he had not then we might never have met at all.'

'I never felt like this about Francisco,' she whispered. 'I didn't even know what love really was.'

The dark eyes searched hers. 'But you feel that you do now?'

'Oh, yes!' Lauren brought up a hand to trace the firm line of his lips with a fingertip, skin tingling to the mere contact. 'You're everything to me, Rafael.'

'So much that you were ready to renounce me not so very long ago.'

'That was my stupid pride getting in the way,' she admitted, and saw a rueful smile touch his lips.

'My own reaction left a lot to be desired. I was angered and hurt by your lack of faith in me, and wanted to wound you in return. Nina Ortega means nothing to me, nor ever has. She made herself available, and I took advantage, no more. Now that I have you, I have no need of such relationships.'

Lauren hesitated before asking the question. 'So why *did* you invite her here the other evening?'

'She was proving difficult to convince that our personal association was over. I intended her to realise that you were the one who had my heart. She brought Ríos with her in the hope of arousing me to jealousy, but my anger was for his presence alone. He is not a man to be trusted.'

'You don't need to tell me,' Lauren assured him softly. 'I don't like him either. If I gave the impression that I might the other day, it was only because I resented the way you reacted.'

'I would find it difficult to change my ways completely,' Rafael acknowledged. 'But I'll do my best to temper my possessiveness.'

His kiss belied the promise, but Lauren was past caring. She wanted to be possessed by this man of hers. Utterly and completely, for all time.

INDULGE A LITTLE 6947 SWEEPSTAKES
NO PURCHASE NECESSARY

HERE'S HOW THE SWEEPSTAKES WORKS:
The Harlequin Reader Service shipments for January, February and March 1994 will contain, respectively, coupons for entry into three prize drawings: a trip for two to San Francisco, an Alaskan cruise for two and a trip for two to Hawaii. To be eligible for any drawing using an Entry Coupon, simply complete and mail according to directions.

There is no obligation to continue as a Reader Service subscriber to enter and be eligible for any prize drawing. You may also enter any drawing by hand printing your name and address on a 3" x 5" card and the destination of the prize you wish that entry to be considered for (i.e., San Francisco trip, Alaskan cruise or Hawaiian trip). Send your 3" x 5" entries to: Indulge a Little 6947 Sweepstakes, c/o Prize Destination you wish that entry to be considered for, P.O. Box 1315, Buffalo, NY 14269-1315, U.S.A. or Indulge a Little 6947 Sweepstakes, P.O. Box 610, Fort Erie, Ontario L2A 5X3, Canada.

To be eligible for the San Francisco trip, entries must be received by 4/30/94; for the Alaskan cruise, 5/31/94; and the Hawaiian trip, 6/30/94. No responsibility is assumed for lost, late or misdirected mail. Sweepstakes open to residents of the U.S. (except Puerto Rico) and Canada, 18 years of age or older. All applicable laws and regulations apply. Sweepstakes void wherever prohibited.

For a copy of the Official Rules, send a self-addressed, stamped envelope (WA residents need not affix return postage) to: Indulge a Little 6947 Rules, P.O. Box 4631, Blair, NE 68009, U.S.A.

INDR93

INDULGE A LITTLE 6947 SWEEPSTAKES
NO PURCHASE NECESSARY

HERE'S HOW THE SWEEPSTAKES WORKS:
The Harlequin Reader Service shipments for January, February and March 1994 will contain, respectively, coupons for entry into three prize drawings: a trip for two to San Francisco, an Alaskan cruise for two and a trip for two to Hawaii. To be eligible for any drawing using an Entry Coupon, simply complete and mail according to directions.

There is no obligation to continue as a Reader Service subscriber to enter and be eligible for any prize drawing. You may also enter any drawing by hand printing your name and address on a 3" x 5" card and the destination of the prize you wish that entry to be considered for (i.e., San Francisco trip, Alaskan cruise or Hawaiian trip). Send your 3" x 5" entries to: Indulge a Little 6947 Sweepstakes, c/o Prize Destination you wish that entry to be considered for, P.O. Box 1315, Buffalo, NY 14269-1315, U.S.A. or Indulge a Little 6947 Sweepstakes, P.O. Box 610, Fort Erie, Ontario L2A 5X3, Canada.

To be eligible for the San Francisco trip, entries must be received by 4/30/94; for the Alaskan cruise, 5/31/94; and the Hawaiian trip, 6/30/94. No responsibility is assumed for lost, late or misdirected mail. Sweepstakes open to residents of the U.S. (except Puerto Rico) and Canada, 18 years of age or older. All applicable laws and regulations apply. Sweepstakes void wherever prohibited.

For a copy of the Official Rules, send a self-addressed, stamped envelope (WA residents need not affix return postage) to: Indulge a Little 6947 Rules, P.O. Box 4631, Blair, NE 68009, U.S.A.

INDR93

INDULGE A LITTLE SWEEPSTAKES

OFFICIAL ENTRY COUPON

This entry must be received by: JUNE 30, 1994
This month's winner will be notified by: JULY 15, 1994
Trip must be taken between: AUGUST 31, 1994-AUGUST 31, 1995

YES, I want to win the 3-Island Hawaiian vacation for two. I understand that the prize includes round-trip airfare, first-class hotels and pocket money as revealed on the "wallet" scratch-off card.

Name ____________________

Address ____________________ Apt. ____________

City ____________________

State/Prov. ____________ Zip/Postal Code ____________

Daytime phone number ____________________
(Area Code)

Account # ____________________

Return entries with invoice in envelope provided. Each book in this shipment has two entry coupons—and the more coupons you enter, the better your chances of winning!

 MONTH3

INDULGE A LITTLE SWEEPSTAKES

OFFICIAL ENTRY COUPON

This entry must be received by: JUNE 30, 1994
This month's winner will be notified by: JULY 15, 1994
Trip must be taken between: AUGUST 31, 1994-AUGUST 31, 1995

YES, I want to win the 3-Island Hawaiian vacation for two. I understand that the prize includes round-trip airfare, first-class hotels and pocket money as revealed on the "wallet" scratch-off card.

Name ____________________

Address ____________________ Apt. ____________

City ____________________

State/Prov. ____________ Zip/Postal Code ____________

Daytime phone number ____________________
(Area Code)

Account # ____________________

Return entries with invoice in envelope provided. Each book in this shipment has two entry coupons—and the more coupons you enter, the better your chances of winning!

© 1993 HARLEQUIN ENTERPRISES LTD. MONTH3